MRS. CATT'S CURIOSITIES

She sells anything and everything — but more than that, she sells hope . . . Ken Weaver has just about hit rock bottom when he comes across Mrs. Catt's Curiosities. And before he knows it, he is leaving the store with a very special purchase . . . But can an old medal really heal a family that has been torn apart? Meanwhile, Jay Randall has spent the better part of a year nursing a broken heart. But thanks to Mrs. Catt and a faded old photograph, he meets a beautiful girl named Cece, and learns to love again.

MONICA BRENT

---◆---

MRS. CATT'S CURIOSITIES

Complete and Unabridged

LINFORD
Leicester

First published in Great Britain in 2013 by
Bookends
London

First Linford Edition
published 2014
by arrangement with
Bookends
London

A catalogue record for this book is available
from the British Library.

ISBN 978–1–4448–2153–6

Published by
F. A. Thorpe (Publishing)
Anstey, Leicestershire

Set by Words & Graphics Ltd.
Anstey, Leicestershire
Printed and bound in Great Britain by
T. J. International Ltd., Padstow, Cornwall

This book is printed on acid-free paper

For Andrea Wilson
and Janet Whitehead,
who made my dreams come true!

Introduction

Milford Circle sits at the centre of Milford city — a mid-sized town, in the centre of a mid-sized state, located at the centre of a mid-sized county. It's a place where middle-class people work hard at their mid-level jobs and bring home their middle-income pay checks. It's not an extraordinary place, and people do not expect the extraordinary to happen . . . not every day, anyway.

The Circle, as it's referred to by its residents, is the heart of the town and the reason people come to visit. At its entrance a roundabout draws cars away from the busy interstate, around an ancient fountain, and onto a charming little street flanked by sycamore trees, cafés, antique shops, and Mrs. Catt's Curiosities.

Mrs. Catt is older than your oldest living relative. She's been in town for years, maybe decades, or perhaps even centuries — no one knows for sure. Her shop is filled with common items, nothing too absurd or unusual, just random. And she has a curious story for every single piece.

There's a bun that sits high upon Mrs. Catt's head, a beautifully coiled silver rope of hair that hasn't lost its shine or lustre, as greying hair often does. Her red glasses are bedazzled with rhinestones and are often hanging around her neck on a beaded chain, making it easy to see the sparkle in her eye. Not everyone who enters her shop leaves with what they came in for, but everyone leaves with an experience they may not have thought they wanted, an experience that stays with them for days and days and niggles at their brain. Leaving Mrs. Catt's shop with anything means something spectacular is about to happen . . . because that's how it works.

Part One

Home is the Hero

1

Ken Weaver thought, *Well I'll be darned*.

He'd lived in Milford almost twenty years. He'd shopped in its stores, eaten in its restaurants and watched movies in its one and only movie theatre. He couldn't even *guess* at how many times he and Lynn had walked the length of Main Street or the hours they'd spent browsing in its shops. But as far as he could recall, he had never come across Mrs. Catt's Curiosities until today.

He'd come into town that early spring Saturday morning more to get out of the house than anything else. He did that more and more these days. He'd always been a quiet, inoffensive man, and he'd enjoyed a quiet, inoffensive life until Fate had revealed other plans for him. Well, for *all* of them, if he was honest about it. And though he tried not to feel sorry for himself — he hated the thought of falling into *that* trap — it was becoming increasingly difficult not to.

So, deciding that distraction was what he needed, he'd driven into town in the hope that a change of scene would improve his mood.

It hadn't.

Although it was now mid-morning, Main Street was about as busy as Main Street ever got — which wasn't very busy at all. It was a street that catered more for tourists than residents, and so it only really came to life during the summer months. Besides, the big stores on the edge of town had all but wiped out their smaller competitors, leaving the centre of Milford more like a wasteland.

That thought alone did little to lighten Ken's already dark disposition, and was, in fact, enough to bring all his pent-up bitterness roaring to the surface.

Life and circumstances changed

whether you wanted them to or not, he reminded himself venomously. You yourself had no say in it. You *never* had any say in it. You worked all your life and did everything the right and best way you could, and when you expected to reap the rewards — nothing grand, mind you, just a nice, comfortable retirement — life kicked you square in the teeth.

It was just then, as his faltering spirits finally hit rock bottom, that he noticed the three diagonal parking spaces outside Mrs. Catt's Curiosities for the very first time. Each one was marked by a different tree, which in itself was odd and suddenly provided him with the distraction he sought. There was a cactus, then a palm, and finally a lemon tree. He realized vaguely that it had been the zesty scent of the lemon tree that had roused him from his melancholy.

He paused, grateful for the diversion, and then turned to examine the store . . . and that was when he thought, *Well, I'll be darned.*

The store window was crowded with all kinds of stuff, from feathered hats and Bakelite butterfly bags, to wind-up robots that doubled as salt-and-pepper shakers and an assortment of dusty hardcover books. There was a tall, mottled mirror in an ornate gilt frame, beneath which a row of mismatched coloured glass bottles stood sentry around a group of tiny Wade figurines. Two curved Civil War-era sabres in remarkable condition lay crossed before them. There was an old Walco Bead Garden Set that evoked memories of his childhood, an untidy stack of joke parking tickets, a selection of men's cufflinks and scarves and even a cute little hatching turtle in porcelain.

Ken shook his head in wonder. Rhinestone sunglasses, candlestick telephones, stuffed owls, dolls in soda bottles . . . was there anything this store *didn't* sell? Mrs. Catt, whoever she was, should have called the place Aladdin's

Cave, because that's sure the way it looked to him.

Then, entirely without warning, he found himself looking not at all the junk piled haphazardly in the window, but at his own reflection in the window itself, and his sudden good humour evaporated immediately.

For there before him stood the semi-transparent, ghostly reflection of a tall, rail-thin man in his early sixties. He wore an open-necked white shirt, a gray sweater and dark pants that were baggy at the knees. This man had short, neatly barbered steel-gray hair and he wore a pair of sober-looking gold-framed spectacles. He had stooped shoulders, a long, tired face, a short nose and fresh-scrubbed, ruddy skin that was just starting to pouch at the corners of his mouth. And his ears! He remembered learning somewhere that the ears and the nose never stopped growing, but when exactly did his own ears begin to resemble those of an African elephant?

If Lynn was here now she'd squeeze

his arm and tell him not to be so hard on himself. But he wasn't being hard on himself, really. He was just seeing as if for the first time just how old and worn down he had become.

All at once he didn't care to be reminded of that, and he turned and started to walk on until the shop's recessed door swung open and a little old lady came outside to squint up at the sunshine.

'It's going to be a lovely morning,' she noted without looking at him. 'Rain later, though. Quite a storm, I believe.'

He nodded, said, 'I guess,' and made to pass on.

'Even so, it's the kind of day that makes you glad to be alive,' she continued, and then added, with peculiar emphasis, 'Or *should* make you glad to be alive.'

There was a hint almost of criticism in her tone that made him stop and look at her. What did she know about him, or his thoughts? he wondered with uncharacteristic belligerence. But even as he asked himself the question he knew the answer. She knew nothing of them, and had simply been passing an innocent comment.

'Yes,' she went on, reaching for the bejewelled glasses that hung from a silver chain around her neck and popping them on, the better to inspect him. 'We have so much to be grateful for, if only we realized it.'

And then, meeting his sad green eyes with her own lively blue ones, she said, very directly, 'I mean, we *know* we're well off, deep down in what we call our heart of hearts, but we don't always *realize* it. We get . . . ' She scowled momentarily, as she sought for the right word, then said: ' . . . *distracted*. Life has a way of doing that, don't you find? Of distracting us from . . . well, from *living*.'

'I guess,' he said again, without noticeable enthusiasm.

It was almost impossible to put an age to this woman — presumably the Mrs. Catt of the sign above the door.

She stood perhaps five feet one — certainly no more — and carried upon her small frame several extra pounds. She wore her silver hair piled high atop her head, which gave the impression of advanced years, and yet when he looked at her face he was surprised by just how youthfully smooth and healthy her skin was. Her eyes were clear and hinted at a wicked sense of humour, and her small, up-tilted nose had been very slightly reddened by the sun, which made her look not unlike the archetypal farmer's wife. She was dressed in a jade-green sweater with a keyhole neck and ribbed cuffs, a pair of pale brown slacks and a pair of tan leather pumps.

'There's no *guess* about it,' she said a little sharply. 'Life is a wonderful thing for the likes of you and I. We have food, we have shelter, we live in a democracy where we can say what we like without fear of reprisal.'

'Well, that's a matter of opinion,' he murmured wryly.

Ignoring him, she went on, 'What do

we *really* have to complain about?'

In his present frame of mind, however, there was something about her sunny outlook that irritated him, and without realizing it he snapped, 'Maybe not everyone's as fortunate as you.'

Startled, she cocked her head, bird-like, and peered up at him.

'I mean,' he stammered, realizing suddenly that he'd spoken out of turn, 'maybe you've been more . . . fortunate . . . than most.'

'I haven't, you know,' she said quietly. 'And you shouldn't presume otherwise.'

'I'm sorry,' he replied stiffly. 'But just maybe *you* shouldn't presume, either.'

She inclined her head, the movement almost regal. 'Then let's start over,' she suggested cheerfully, and before he knew it she had looped one of her arms through one of his and was leading him into the store.

Too startled to resist, Ken saw that he'd been right — the place *was* an Aladdin's cave.

Mrs. Catt's stock — if such it could be called — was . . . *diverse*, to say the least. A stuffed moose head surveyed the chaos from its position high on the left-hand wall. And what chaos! In his first slightly bewildered glance Ken saw a set of mismatched skis propped in one corner, just behind an old player piano, followed by a wicker basket filled to brimming with age-worn arrowheads; a pile of reclaimed bricks; a stack of hubcaps; a Viking helmet; a shelf filled with candles of different heights, shapes, colours, scents and thicknesses; a bird house; a selection of clocks; a jumble of baking dishes; an enormous clam shell; three music boxes; a pile of brooches shaped like lobsters and poodles; and an extended family of Russian dolls.

He didn't think it was possible to cram so much stuff into so relatively small a space, and yet, much as he hated to admit it, there was something curiously cosy to the store that gave him his first real release from the frustrations of the day. To his surprise he saw the store more as a sanctuary than anything else. But a sanctuary from his own home life? A home life he had always previously valued above all else?

If that was true, then he realized just how low he had fallen.

'Now,' said Mrs. Catt, shuffling around the glass counter and pausing beside a beaded curtain that presumably led through to private quarters at the rear. 'Can I get you a cup of herbal tea while you browse?'

'Oh, I'm not — '

'Nonsense,' interrupted Mrs. Catt. 'Of course you want to browse. And why wouldn't you? You know that phrase, 'Something for everyone?' Well, I like to put it another way. I always say that *everything* has a *someone*. How many items do you suppose I have in my . . . well, what shall we call it? Stock? Inventory?'

'I don't really — '

'No, of course you don't, silly,'

chided Mrs. Catt. 'It was a rhetorical question. That means it didn't really need a reply.'

Ken's lips thinned. He must look dumb indeed if she thought he needed to have *that* explained to him.

'But my point,' she continued happily, 'is that every single thing you see here before you, from the lowliest piece to the most expensive item — which, incidentally, is a Prince Edward Island Stamp from 1872, upon the back of which someone with far more ability than I has inscribed the entire *Rubáiyát of Omar Khayyám* — is wanted by someone. They might not know it at the time, of course, but they know it when they see it.'

Again she cocked her head at him. 'Have you seen what *you* want yet?'

'I — '

'No,' she said, 'of course you haven't. That's because I've been chattering on and haven't yet allowed you to peruse those wonders I am pleased to call my curiosities. So — ' And here she patted him on the forearm. ' — you have a little look around while I make our tea.'

'There's no need — '

'There's *always* need for a nice cup of herbal tea,' she interrupted, adding, as if it should mean something, 'It's Roobios tea. It comes from South Africa and it has a rather pleasant malty taste. I think you'll like it.' And again she fixed him with that very direct look of hers. 'It's excellent for lifting the mood.'

Without another word, she bustled through the beaded curtain, humming pleasantly as she went.

Ken looked after her and once again shook his head. Mrs. Catt really was one of the strangest women he had ever met.

For a moment he considered leaving the store while she was otherwise engaged. He had no great desire to socialize over tea, and certainly not with a woman who didn't seem to appreciate his misfortunes.

And yet she was right. Even now he

17

supposed things could have been worse. It was difficult to imagine *how*, certainly . . . but he was at least willing to concede the possibility.

Standing there in the middle of the store, surrounded by all kinds of clutter, he listened to the sounds she made preparing tea. Cups and saucers clattered. A kettle began to whistle like an approaching train. There was a rattle that he translated as cookies being slid from packet to plate.

Ken didn't want the woman to make him too welcome: then he might feel obliged to buy something, and what could possibly interest him here?

As Mrs. Catt turned from humming to singing softly, he knew that he would never get a better chance to escape than now. It might be ungallant, but he reckoned he could live with that.

He turned and started for the door, but pulled up sharp when he saw a black cat barring his way. The cat had obviously just wandered in off the street and now planted itself in the doorway.

With sudden, ridiculous urgency, Ken tried to shoo the animal away, but since it clearly had no intention of getting out of his path he decided to step over it.

At the very last moment, however, the cat darted out from under his feet and blurred across the store to vanish into the back room. Startled, Ken lost his footing and grabbed for a free-standing set of shelves to steady himself. The shelves wobbled a little, then righted themselves again — but not before a little red box about the size and thickness of a cigarette packet tumbled off the top shelf and dropped toward the floor.

More by accident than design, Ken snatched for the box and caught it before it could land against the worn linoleum.

He was just about to put it back on the shelf when something about it struck him as being . . . *familiar*, somehow.

Suddenly piqued, his forgot all about making his surreptitious getaway and instead gently pulled back the hinged lid, knowing — but not really knowing how he knew — what he would find inside.

He was right.

Nestled against red velvet sat a medal.

It wasn't *the* medal, of course. At least he didn't *think* so. That would be pushing coincidence way beyond the bounds of possibility. And yet these things didn't exactly grow on trees . . .

'Impressive, isn't it?'

Mrs. Catt's voice, coming from close beside him, made him jump and snap the lid shut.

He had no idea how she could have snuck up on him so quietly. He turned and saw her peering up at him, eyes clear and seemingly innocent behind her glasses. And yet he had the weirdest notion that she had been privy to all the memories that had just flickered across the movie screen of his mind, and the thought made him feel strangely vulnerable.

'Here you are,' she said, and plucking the medal and box from his fingers she handed him his cup of herbal tea. 'It's the Silver Star,' she said.

'Yes, I know.'

'You have to do something pretty special to earn one of these,' she went on.

He cleared his throat and asked hesitantly, 'Where, uh . . . where did you get it?'

She looked off into the distance, clearly casting her mind back. After a moment, she shook her head. 'I honestly can't remember. Maybe I bought it as part of a collection. Why?'

'It's just . . . '

'Yes?'

He shrugged. 'I never thought to see one again, that's all.'

'Oh?' Mrs. Catt turned and bustled back toward the counter, where Ken noticed she had left her own cup of tea and a small plate piled high with cookies — actually, strawberry cheese-cake brownies, his favourites. But how

21

had she known that? Or was that just another coincidence?

'Was it yours?' she asked, holding up the small medal box. 'Did you lose it, or something?'

'No, not mine. It belonged to my son-in-law.'

'You must be very proud.'

Before he could stop himself he said bitterly, 'I would have been prouder still if it hadn't been awarded *posthumously.*'

At once Mrs. Catt's expression transformed, and there was so much compassion in the way she looked at him that it was almost shocking.

'How much are you asking for it?' he said, almost gruffly.

Mrs. Catt said, 'I don't really *know*. I mean, they're uncommon items.'

He thought cynically, *Oh, here it comes. Now she's going to stiff me on the price.*

She opened the box and studied the medal thoughtfully for a long, long moment. Considering that it was the third-highest combat decoration awarded by the United States, coming after the Medal of Honour and the service crosses, the five-pointed star itself was remarkably small, measuring no more than one and a half inches from tip to tip. A smaller star sat at its centre, surrounded by an engraved laurel wreath and a series of outward-fanning rays. It was attached to a rectangular-shaped ribbon with a central red stripe against a white background, and two blue stripes of different thicknesses running down either edge. On the reverse was inscribed the words FOR GALLANTRY IN ACTION.

At last the old woman broke her long silence.

'Would you say ten dollars was fair?' she asked.

Ken's jaw almost dropped open. A medal like this . . . well, he had no real idea of its worth, but he knew it must be worth a lot more than that.

Anyone else might have leapt at the chance to snap up such a bargain, but it went against Ken's do-right nature. 'I'd say it was very fair — to me. But not especially fair to you, Mrs. Catt.'

'Well, I'd be happy with ten dollars.' She raised her cup and smiled. She had a very radiant smile, he thought. 'So . . . shall we drink to it? And perhaps indulge ourselves with these rather tempting brownies?'

He smiled too — the first time that day.

That week.

That month.

'We shall indeed,' he said, his mood brightening suddenly.

2

As soon as it was polite to do so, Ken left the store and hurried back to his car, a Toyota Prius he'd parked on a tree-lined side street a few blocks south. As he settled himself behind the wheel he took out the small box and examined the medal again, thrilled with his purchase and unable to remember the last time he'd felt so exhilarated.

Instinctively, however, he cautioned himself against building his hopes too high. For just a moment there he had allowed himself to think that this medal, this chance find, might solve all their problems.

Well, he might be naïve, but he wasn't *that* naïve.

Gloom draped itself over him again, and he tried as he always did to fight it off. Still, you never knew. Just maybe today's unexpected find *would* be enough to enable them all to make a fresh start.

The drive home took a little less than twenty minutes, and as had become his habit over the past several months, Ken reluctantly but somehow obsessively found himself remembering yet again everything that had brought him to his present sorry state.

He'd never seen it coming. Who would? Who ever lives their life in the expectation that somehow it's all going to be derailed? And yet that's exactly what had happened to the Weavers.

They'd never been what you might call *comfortable*, but they'd never been poor, either. They'd gotten by without too much of a struggle, and their daughter, Sarah, had wanted for nothing. Life had been good, with no particular upsets to rock their metaphorical boat.

When Sarah had started dating Mike Nelson at high school, Ken and Lynn couldn't have been happier. The kids

had known each other since kindergar-
ten. A year or so older than Sarah, Mike
was a good-looking, nice-natured lad
with a mop of corn-yellow hair and just
about the clearest, bluest eyes Ken had
ever seen on a boy.

Mike's parents were good folks,
well-liked and well-respected in their
little corner of suburbia, and the
relationship between Sarah and Mike
had always been close — so much so
that it had always seemed to Ken that
they were somehow carrying on a
relationship that had actually started in
some previous life. It was the only way
he could explain it.

Anyway, it surprised no one when
their friendship eventually blossomed
into something much more. The only
surprise was that it took as long as it
did for Sarah and Mike to realize the
true depth of their feeling for each
other.

They'd dated, they'd gotten engaged,
and on Sarah's eighteenth birthday
they'd married. And when their son,

Ryan, was born about a year later, Ken became just about the proudest grandfather anyone had ever seen. He doted on Ryan, and Ryan in return grew into a happy, chuckling little boy who loved nothing more than spending all the time he could with his 'Gramps'.

Two years after that Mike fulfilled his long-held dream of going into the military. His larger-than-life grandfather, Jared Nelson, had served in the 101st Airborne, the so-called 'Screaming Eagles,' and Mike had grown up listening to stories of his granddad's exploits. Thus, he had decided early on that he wanted to follow in old Jared's footsteps. So when Mike enlisted in the 4th Infantry, Sarah became an army bride, and Ryan an army brat.

Life had been a whirlwind for them then, but despite their busy lives the kids still got home as often as they could and their visits were always a pleasure. As for Mike . . . well, army life suited him down to the ground and he went from strength to strength. The 4th

Infantry, known as the Ivy Division (it was a play on the Roman numeral *IV*, meaning four), had a long and proud history, having seen action in both World Wars, Vietnam and Iraq. It was widely regarded as one of the most technically and tactically proficient divisions in America's army, and because he'd always been bright and eager to learn, Mike quickly climbed the ranks to become Sergeant First Class.

Then he got sent to Afghanistan.

As Ken remembered that period, his hands tightened on the steering wheel until his knuckles turned white.

Of course, you always worry when you have someone in the armed forces and they're deployed to somewhere like that. But likewise there's always part of you that hopes and believes that the worst is never going to happen. It *can't* — your mind just won't allow you to consider it because it is simply *beyond* consideration.

And so, when the worst *does* happen,

there's a sense of . . . unreality to it, as if you're the victim of a very bad joke.

But it isn't a joke. It's real.

Mike had been out on patrol in a remote part of eastern Afghanistan when a roadside bomb had exploded, injuring three civilians. Mike and his men, in an armoured personnel carrier nearby, saw it happen and went to help, inadvertently detonating a second, larger bomb in the process.

Mike and two of the soldiers with him were killed.

Killed . . .

Sarah, of course, was devastated by the news. There was some kind of mistake, surely? This kind of thing . . . it always happened to somebody *else*. And Ryan . . . well, it still broke Ken's heart to see that look of complete incomprehension on Ryan's face when he had taken the boy into his room and told him, as best he could, why he wasn't going to see his father ever again.

The family's subsequent contact with

the army, the flying home of the body, the pomp and ceremony of the military funeral with its honour guard, the folding and presentation of the flag and the mournful playing of 'Taps' by a single bugler, followed by the presentation to Sarah of Mike's posthumous Purple Heart and Silver Star . . . they all did their bit to reinforce the awful reality of their situation. Even now, Ken wasn't completely sure how his daughter had made it through the funeral in one piece.

After the presentation of the medals, Sarah took to wearing Mike's Purple Heart as a pendant. Aside from memories, all Ryan had to remember Mike by was his Silver Star.

Now, driving through the pleasant suburbs where he and Lynn had bought their one-storey ranch-style retirement home, Ken quickly blinked the threat of tears from his eyes. He'd gone fifty years without shedding a single one. Now sometimes all it took was a weather bulletin to bring a lump to his throat.

But it wasn't Mike's death that had turned their world upside down, though goodness knew that had been bad enough. It was the effect it had had upon Sarah and, more especially, Ryan.

It was as well, he thought, that he reached home when he did, because he really didn't want to think any more about the way things had gone, not right then.

Instead, as he climbed out of the car and headed across the lawn for the front door, he turned his thoughts back to the medal, and found himself hoping against hope that it would somehow be enough to turn their lousy lives around.

3

Even before he let himself through the front door, Ken heard the dull, insistent thump-thump-thump of heavy metal music coming from Ryan's room. Immediately he thinned his lips and shook his head, but once again reminded himself that he shouldn't really blame the boy. He might now be twelve, but Ryan was still a kid. And Ken guessed he was reacting the only way he could to the way his life had turned out — by rebelling.

Lynn was in the kitchen, a pale-faced, slim woman of average height who wore her shoulder-length light auburn hair with a centre part. With wide-set hazel eyes beneath fine, arched brows, she was still handsome but now, like Ken himself, undeniably age-worn. But when she looked up and saw the animation in his expression it somehow communicated itself to her, and pushing away from the worktop, where she'd been preparing vegetables for their evening meal, she said urgently, 'What is it, Ken? What's happened?'

He wanted to say, 'A miracle.' But instead he said, 'You'll never guess what I picked up in town.'

Without waiting for her to guess — which she never would, anyway — he took the box out of his pocket and set it down on the worktop between them, then opened the lid.

Lynn looked down at the medal, the skin at the bridge of her pert little nose puckering. 'Where on earth did you find that?' she asked in a breathless hush.

'A little curio shop. Mrs. Catt's Curiosities.'

'Never heard of it.'

'Neither had I, till this morning. Anyway, I went inside, had a look around and was just about to leave when I spotted this.'

'I dread to think how much it cost.'

'Ten dollars.'

Her eyes widened. 'Is that *all?*'

'Oh, the old girl, Mrs. Catt, knew it was probably worth a whole lot more. But when I accidentally let slip that Mike . . . well, she said she was happy with the price.'

'Oh, Ken . . . '

'I know. What are the chances, huh?' He grinned stupidly, then sobered just as quickly. 'It's a sign,' he whispered. And there — he'd said what he'd been thinking ever since he saw it. 'I'm sure it is, Lynn.'

Lynn's brown eyes moved briefly toward the direction of Ryan's room. 'When are you going to give it to him?' she asked.

'Right now.'

He scooped up the medal, closed the lid and left the kitchen.

Following Mike's death, Ryan had become withdrawn and uncommunicative, and had never again shown the affection that had always previously been so much a part of him. In a way,

Ken felt that the boy had blamed him for his father's death, because he, Ken, had been the one to break the terrible news. Or maybe Ryan had withdrawn into himself as a defence mechanism — that by distancing himself from his family he would never have to go through the pain of loss ever again.

But it soon became more than that. The boy seemed to develop a belligerent streak, and discarded all respect for authority. Perhaps he didn't blame Ken for Mike's death — perhaps he blamed the whole wide world.

When it had become clear that Sarah was finding it harder and harder to cope with him, Ken and Lynn had suggested that maybe it would be better if they all moved in together. Maybe that way they could somehow recreate the family unit that had been torn apart by Mike's death.

Unfortunately, in the move, Sarah had somehow lost Mike's Silver Star.

It was impossible to know how it had happened. With her mind elsewhere, it was a wonder that Sarah could concentrate on even the simplest task, much less a house-move. But Ryan didn't see it that way. He had blamed Sarah for losing the medal, claiming that it showed just how important Mike had really been to her.

After that the situation had only deteriorated. They had all tried to understand Ryan, they had all tried to make allowances for him, but in return Ryan had only abused and taken advantage of them. In so doing, he had turned what should have been Ken and Lynn's peaceful retirement into a nightmare, and slowly but surely he had worn all of them down.

Now, as he approached the room that had become Ryan's private, keep-out-or-else domain, Ken grimaced at the sound of the heavy metal music that hammered from within. His neighbour, Jim Mullen, had already spoken to him about the noise, and Ken had assured him that he'd have a word with Ryan. He had, too. But Ryan had spent the two years since his father's death believing that the world owed him something, and wasn't about to back down for anyone.

Ken knocked at the door. There was no response. Ryan probably didn't even hear him. He knocked a little louder. Still there was no answer. Reaching a decision, he twisted the handle and went inside.

Ryan's room was a mess, the walls plastered with posters of bands with names like Anthrax, Blue Cheer, Fallout, Grave Digger and Kickaxe. Ryan himself was stretched out on his unmade bed, slamming at the air above him with imaginary drumsticks. He looked around and glared at Ken, showing nothing of the warmth, the love, the happiness that used to be so obvious in him.

'Can I have a word?' Ken called above the pounding music.

'What?'

'I said, can I have . . . ' He glanced meaningfully at the CD player in the corner. 'Can you turn that down for a moment?'

The boy looked up at him. He seemed so much older than his years. When he made no move to comply, Ken mimed turning down an invisible volume button and with an exaggerated rolling of his clear blue eyes — eyes that always used to remind Ken so much of Mike's — Ryan snatched up the remote and softened the music.

'Happy now?' the boy asked.

Ken was used to his hostility and almost complete lack of respect. Like everything else about the situation, it hadn't always been that way. At first Ken had tried to set the boy right, to remind him to show a little consideration for his elders. But trying to reason with Ryan was like trying to count the grains of sand on a beach — impossible and seemingly pointless.

'I wanted you to see something,' Ken said, crossing the room. 'All right if I sit down?'

Ryan shrugged. He was tall for his

age, and lean, just like his dad. His hair was the vibrant colour of straw, his face round, eyes far older than they should be. A pale bridge of freckles spanned his snub nose. His mouth was thin, and had grown unused to smiling.

Ken set his weight down gently on the edge of the mattress. 'I've got something for you,' he said. 'Something I think you might like.'

'Tickets for the next Sweet Savage gig?' Ryan asked sarcastically.

'Better than that,' said Ken. 'Here.'

He held out the medal box. Ryan looked at it with a hint of suspicion. 'What is it?' he asked.

'Why don't you open it and find out?'

'Why don't you just tell me and save us both the hassle?'

Ken stared at him, biting back a retort that he knew would only make things worse.

At last the boy sighed and pushed himself up onto one elbow. He took the box from Ken and Ken watched him, acutely aware of his pulses racing in expectation of Ryan's reaction. Ryan looked at the box, then opened it and stared down at the medal.

'You know what it is, of course,' said Ken, when the boy made no comment.

'Sure I know what it is.'

'Well, it's yours now.'

'Is it the one my mom lost when we came to live here?'

'I don't know. It could be.'

'But it might *not* be.'

'Ryan, I can't say one way or the other. All I know is that these medals don't exactly grow on trees. It might be the same one. But even if it's not . . . well, a replacement's better than nothing, right?'

Ryan shrugged one shoulder . . . and handed the medal back.

'It's for *you*, son,' said Ken gently.

'What do *I* want with it?'

'I thought you'd be pleased — '

'Why?' asked the boy. 'What do I want with somebody else's medal? What do I want with *any* medal?'

'It's a reminder of your dad . . . '

41

'It's a reminder of how clumsy my mom is,' Ryan countered venomously. 'She goes on all the time about how much he meant to her, but when it came to it she couldn't even keep hold of his medal.'

'She didn't lose it on purpose, Ry.'

'So she said. But I gave it to her for safekeeping. I *gave* it to her because it meant a lot to me — and still she lost it.'

Ken's normally placid temperament finally flared. 'Maybe you don't understand the way it was, Ry. Your mom had other things on her mind. She was hurting; she just wasn't thinking straight. I know it's not much consolation, but . . . well, sometimes things *get* lost.'

'Yeah — but not things that're supposed to *mean* something, that're supposed to be *important*. But I guess it shows what she really thought about my dad — and me.'

'Your mother loves you, Ry. We *all* do.'

'Well, I don't want your crummy medal,' said the boy. 'Here, take it back.'

Ken looked at him as if he was a stranger . . . and that's exactly what he was, what he had become. What did it take to get through to him?

Dumbly he took the proffered box back and stood up. 'I thought you'd be pleased,' he said.

'I guess you thought wrong.'

Ken's expression hardened. 'I guess I did. I thought you'd like to have it, if only for what it represents.'

'And what's that?'

'A reward . . . no, not reward, an *acknowledgement*, of what your dad gave . . . what he sacrificed . . . for the country he loved.'

'Yippee,' muttered the boy.

Knowing he wasn't going to get anywhere with him, Ken crossed the room to the door. Behind him Ryan pressed a button on the remote and the music came up, louder and even more obnoxious than before.

'I'll leave it here,' Ken said, lifting his voice again and gesturing to a chest of drawers beside the door, 'in case you change your mind.'

But he might just as well have been talking to himself. As far as Ryan was concerned, Ken had already left the room.

4

Ken closed the door softly behind him and sagged. He'd really convinced himself that the medal might turn Ryan around. But all he'd had instead was another disappointment. And added to that, the prospect of a continuation of this miserable life that was no life at all.

Suddenly the unfairness of it all overwhelmed him. Two years . . . For two unrelenting years he'd tried to be there for Sarah and Ryan and Lynn. He'd written off all the plans he'd made for his long-awaited, hobby-filled retirement and resigned himself to this new existence — it could hardly be called a life — and always he'd bolstered himself with the thought that it wouldn't always be this way; that somewhere down the line something would happen, it was *bound* to; that they would all come out of it and things would be happy again, as they used to be.

But now, when he recalled that hostile, old-before-his-time look in Ryan's eyes, he realized that a resolution to this thing was never going to happen, *never* —

Without warning his chin suddenly hit his chest and he began to sob, fighting against it all the while but knowing it was a battle he could no longer win. He tried to keep his sobbing muffled, at least until he could make it to the bathroom, but even as he turned and stumbled blindly along the hallway he heard a sound behind him and looked around, almost guiltily.

Lynn was watching him from the far end of the hallway, her expression so filled with compassion that it only increased his misery, and all at once he let it come, a series of great, shoulder-wracking sobs.

Eyes squeezed shut, he felt Lynn come to him, hold him, hug him, lead him into their bedroom and close the door softly behind them. He went docilely, suddenly too tired to do anything but go where he was led. Then she put her hands on his shoulders and forced him to sit on the bed, and knelt before him and studied him through troubled eyes as he dragged a handkerchief from his pocket, took off his glasses, dabbed at his eyes, and blew his nose.

'I'm sorry,' he said, voice hitching. 'I didn't mean — '

'You've nothing to apologize for,' she assured him, taking his free hand and squeezing it. 'I take it Ryan was less than grateful?'

He shrugged. 'It's n-not that . . . '

'I know,' said Lynn. 'It's everything. But it can't go on like this, Ken. It's going to make you ill.' *It already has*, she thought wretchedly.

'I j-just wish we could sort this thing out,' he managed, his voice sounding like that of a lost and frightened child.

47

'We can,' she said. 'With a little plain speaking.'

He stared at her, horrified. 'We can't do that.'

'Why not?'

'Sarah's been through enough. And so has the boy. We can't make things any harder for them.'

'But Ryan can make things harder for us, is that it?'

'You know that's not what I mean. I'm just afraid that, if we come down too hard on them . . . they're fragile.'

'They won't break,' she said.

'No. But they might get the idea that we're somehow sick of having them around.'

'I know,' she said tiredly.

They'd been over this a million times before. Mike's death had somehow numbed Sarah to the world around her. She held herself together — just — but losing Mike had broken her emotionally, and Ken and Lynn were at a loss as to know how to repair the damage. Worse, she took all the guilt for Ryan's increasingly belligerent behaviour on herself and tried to make excuses for him, as if he had every right to behave the way he did simply because he had lost his father.

At all costs, Ken and Lynn wanted to stand by the pair of them. But things couldn't go on the way they were. And if they tried to bring things to a head . . . well, there was the very real danger that they might alienate Sarah and Ryan altogether, and then things would only be worse still.

But *something* had to be said and done to resolve things once and for all. The only question was . . . what?

* * *

In his room, Ryan found his eyes wandering to the cabinet where his grandfather had left the medal. Just the thought of it made him snort. What planet did that guy come from? Did Gramps *really* think that giving him a lousy medal could make up for the loss

49

of his dad? Was he *really* that dumb?

All at once his temper blazed — it did that all the time, lately — and he launched himself up off the bed and marched across the room. He snatched the little box off the cabinet and tore the lid back. He stared down at the medal, mixed emotions warring within him. On the one hand he knew he should be grateful that he had *something*, at least, to remember his dad by. Like Gramps had said, this was recognition for what he'd sacrificed. But on the other hand the sight of it infuriated him. Was this all his dad's life was worth? A lousy hunk of metal?

He snapped the lid shut and went to the window, opened it and then threw the box out as far as it would go, watching with a perverse sense of satisfaction as it hit a thick yellow bush at front corner of the property and then tumbled between the foliage. Let it stay there, and rot!

He hopped back onto the bed, wanting to feel that he's scored some kind of victory over his grandfather but knowing only a curious sense of emptiness. For a moment he almost felt sorry for his grandfather. Gramps had only given him the medal in the first place because he'd thought it might —

But he stopped that thought right where it was. He didn't want to see things from anyone else's point of view. The only point of view that mattered was *his*. It took more effort that he cared to admit, but he forced all that hostility to come back to the fore and he wore it like a suit of armour, because just like armour it would protect him from any more hurt.

He was seized by a sudden restlessness. He didn't want to be in this room or this house any more. He wanted to get out of here and find someplace that was all his own, where no one else could hassle him — and he knew just where to go.

He got up, switched off the CD player with a flick of the remote, then grabbed his cell, shoved it into his pants pocket and went out into the hallway. He could hear Gramps and Gramma talking softly in their bedroom. Probably dissing him. He headed for the door, seeing no need to let them know that he was going out, or where.

Deep down, though, it hurt him to treat them so badly. But he did it and kept doing it because in some weird way he really wanted to hurt himself. So once again he stifled any feelings of remorse and replaced them with disdain, and opened the front door, determined to get out of here before another minute passed into history.

But it didn't work out like that, because a man was blocking his way, his right hand just lifting to ring the doorbell.

And in his left —

Ryan felt a stab or surprise.

In his left he held the medal box.

5

For a moment they looked at each other. The man was tall and wide-shouldered, wearing an unbuttoned plaid shirt over a white tee, well-worn jeans and tan boots. Parked at the curb behind him was a beat-up Toyota Land Cruiser in firebrick red. Ryan hadn't heard it pull up.

Ryan eyed the man suspiciously. He wasn't as old as Gramps, but he *was* old — at least thirty. He had a long, lean face and casually finger-combed blond hair. He looked back at Ryan through mild blue eyes that held a permanent squint, then showed even teeth in a grin and held out the medal box.

'I think you lost somethin',' he said.

He sounds like some kind of hick, Ryan thought.

He continued to eye the stranger suspiciously and made no move to take the box. 'I don't think so.'

The newcomer raised his sandy eyebrows. 'This is yours, right?'

'No.'

'I found it right outside your house.'

'Doesn't mean to say it's mine,' said Ryan, his tone matching his surly expression. 'Any case — '

He bit off abruptly.

'Any case what?' asked the man.

'Nothing.'

He was going to say, *Any case, I saw where it landed. In that yellow bush. No way you could have seen it from the sidewalk.*

'Well, I reckon it belongs here, right enough,' the man decided sociably.

'Why's that?'

'Your name Nelson, son? Ryan Nelson?'

'Who wants to know?'

The stranger smiled. 'You don't try awful hard to make friends, do you?'

Ryan shrugged. 'It's not my medal. I don't know anything about it. If you found it why don't you just keep it?'

'Who said anythin' about it bein' a medal?'

The softly voiced question left Ryan flummoxed. But fortunately for him distraction arrived at that moment in the shape of Ken and Lynn, who had been drawn by the sound of voices.

'Can I help you?' asked Ken, hoping it didn't look obvious that he'd been crying.

Before the newcomer could reply, Ryan took advantage of the moment, muttered, 'I'm outta here,' and then pushed past the man in the doorway and hurried around the side of the house.

The man watched him go for just a second, then turned back to Ken and Lynn. His eyes met with Ken's and he frowned briefly when he saw the bloodshot look in them, suspected its cause and then said quietly, 'I'm sorry to call right out of the blue. I'm lookin' for Sarah Nelson.'

'Sarah's not home right now. She's at work.'

'Too bad. You're Sarah's folks, I guess?'

'Uh-huh.'

'I'm Jack Donovan. I served with Mike in Helmand.' He offered his hand. It was big and callused, a hand used to hard physical work. 'You had a heck of a son-in-law there, folks.'

Startled, Ken shook with Jack. 'You *knew* Mike?'

'Never knew anyone finer.'

Ryan reappeared again, this time astride his Raleigh Mountain Scout. He cycled away without a backward look.

'Please,' said Lynn, 'come in, Mr. Donovan. Sarah shouldn't be more than a half-hour or so. She works half-days on Saturdays down at Peebles.'

'Thanks,' said Donovan. 'And call me Jack, why don't you?' As he stepped through the door, he held the box out to Ken. 'I guess this must be yours.'

Ken stared at it. 'Where did you find it?'

'Out in the street. I reckon you must have dropped it.'

Ken knew better, but said only, 'Yeah, I reckon I must've.'

They went into the living room and Lynn hurried through to the kitchen to fetch coffee and cookies.

'You knew Mike well?' asked Ken.

'Well enough. He was a good man to have around in a tight fix . . . and there were plenty of those where we were.'

'That I can believe. You boys are doing a hell of a job out there.'

'Thank you, sir.'

'Are you on leave?'

Jack quirked a brief smile. 'Something like that. I got home a while back, but this is the first chance I've had to look up Mike's folks. I wanted to tell them what a great guy he was; how he held us all together when things got hairy. 'Course, they already knew he was the best, but sometimes it's nice to hear it from someone else.'

'And you wanted to tell Sarah the same thing?'

'Sarah and Ryan both, yessir,' replied Jack.

'Well, I think they could both stand to hear it,' said Lynn, coming back into the room. 'They took the news hard, the pair of them, but that thing they say about time being a great healer? It's not working in their case. It'll be good for them to talk to someone who knew Mike so well . . . you know, out in the field, I mean.'

Jack nodded and glanced toward the window, as if suddenly seeking distraction from that earlier time. 'You got a nice-lookin' grandson there,' he remarked. 'Mike would be proud of the way he's growin' up.'

Before he could stop himself, Ken said, 'I doubt that, somehow.'

'Oh?'

'Well, you met him. He isn't exactly a candidate for sainthood.'

'Not many of us are, Mr. Weaver.'

'I suppose. But . . . well, no matter. He lost his dad and it turned him upside down and inside out. But he'll

work through it eventually, I daresay.'

Ken's tone, however, said he doubted that very much.

★ ★ ★

It was weird, Ryan thought. Up here, in the woods far above town, was the only place he ever really knew peace. He wasn't especially interested in the flora or the fauna. He was still at the age when he thought that kind of stuff was dumb, the province of nerds and geeks. But as soon as he left town behind him and the blacktop yielded to an unmade lane that crunched beneath his spinning tires, it felt almost like he was going home.

Not that it was so hard to under-stand, he guessed. He didn't like it where he was. Correction: he *hated* it where he was. He hated living with his mom and grandparents. They didn't understand him, didn't understand the way he felt. How could they? But that didn't stop them from treating him like a kid, as if they somehow knew him better than he knew himself.

Out here, though, in the vast sprawl of these wooded hills, he could actually *be* himself. There was no one here to judge him or tell him who he should be. Up here was . . . heck, it sounded kind of dumb to admit it even to himself, but up here he found some kind of *acceptance*.

He soon left the roadway behind and cycled up through glades of black tupelo, its scarlet and purple foliage long since shed and new green growth now budding on its outspread branches; then on past red pine and conical pin oaks, whose branches draped down around them in such a way that made them look as if they were wearing skirts.

Eventually the wheatgrass grew so thick and tufty that he had to dismount and push his bike. In the branches overhead thrushes and robins, warblers, cardinals, tanagers and sparrows provided a pleasant soundtrack that was a world away from the heavy metal music he favoured at home.

He'd heard that black and brown bears roamed these slopes, but he'd never seen any. Same with bobcats. But he *had* spotted the tracks of white-tailed deer on occasion, and even moose and coyotes on his numerous visits to these high, isolated spaces . . . so he guessed he must've absorbed more about the flora and fauna than he realized.

Cottontail rabbits gambolled together in a sunlit clearing. Forgetting his troubles momentarily, he paused to watch them and grinned the kind of grin his gramps could now only recall as a dim and distant memory. Squirrels darted up and around tree trunks to further entertain the boy.

Presently he came to a shallow stream trickling between steep, shale-covered banks, and followed it deeper into a green gloom created by a network of low-hanging branches. Moss grew thick on large, spilled boulders, and the place took on a mysterious air that he had always found secretly thrilling. In his mind he was an explorer, going where no man had gone before him. Not that he really believed that for one second, of course, but this place never failed to inspire a sense of adventure and discovery in him.

At last he reached his destination, a dark, ragged hole set high in the side of the steepest bank. Beyond it lay a cave with a low ceiling and craggy, uneven limestone walls. He set his bike against one of these, then found himself a spot a little further back and sank gratefully to the dusty floor. He wondered how many hours he'd spent here in the past, just listening to the cries of birds above the soothing chuckle of the stream, and watching tiny spiders weave intricate webs while colourful millipedes made their way from A to B in a series of the most perfect and unhurried flexings.

His friends would think he was dumb. But they didn't have the problems he had; they didn't need to find some kind of sanctuary to keep themselves sane.

He looked around with a sense of deep satisfaction. This cave — *his* cave — was the closest thing he had to a real home. One of these days he was going to live here for good and never, ever go back down to civilization.

★　★　★

Soon Ken and Lynn were chatting to Jack Donovan as if they were old friends. Jack told them he came from the Texas Hill Country, where his father still ran the family ranch, the Circle D, which was situated midway between Del Rio and Sonora. It was good, clean, open country, he said, a world away from the heat and dust of Afghanistan.

'Now, why aren't I surprised to hear that?' asked Lynn.

Jack frowned at her. 'About Afghanistan?'

'About the ranch,' she replied.

'You've got cowboy stamped all over you.'

'Well, maybe not so much anymore,' Jack muttered softly.

For a while, listening to him, Ken felt his dark mood easing. Here was a decent, God-fearing man who, like Mike, had gone away to fight for his country. Unlike Mike, he had made it back home, and he got the impression that what Jack had experienced overseas had somehow changed but by no means embittered him; if anything, it had given him a greater perspective on life.

At last they heard Sarah's green 2001 Honda Fit pull up outside, and then the slam of a car door. Lynn said, 'Ah, here she is at last.'

Jack rose expectantly to his feet.

The front door opened and a moment later Sarah came in, pulling up sharp when she saw that her parents had a visitor.

Sarah was tall and willowy, with side-parted dark strawberry-blonde hair worn to just below shoulder-length.

Her skin was flawless and a very delicate pink, her brows thin and arched above teal-blue eyes. She had a straight nose with flared nostrils, a wide mouth and cheeks that would dimple whenever she smiled. But she didn't smile. In fact, she looked almost shocked to find Jack there.

'I'm sorry,' she said at last. 'I didn't mean to — '

'Jack's here to see *you*,' said her mother.

Sarah slowly came forward and studied Jack more closely. 'I'm sorry, have we met before?'

'No, ma'am,' he said.

'Jack served in Helmand alongside Mike,' Ken explained softly.

He caught Lynn's eye then, and Lynn, getting the message, said, 'Come and help me make some fresh coffee, Ken.'

They left the suddenly silent room.

6

At last Jack broke the heavy silence.

'I'm sorry to show up unannounced,' he said, 'but like I told your parents, Mike and I were pretty tight, and I just came from visitin' his folks.'

'How . . . how are they?' asked Sarah. 'We talk once a week or so, but . . . '

But, she thought, *we seem to talk less and less as the weeks go by, and now it seems more like we're strangers than in-laws.*

'They're fine,' he said. 'They asked to be remembered to you. It was them who told me where to find you.'

'Please,' she said, flustering a little because she had grown distant and unused to company, 'sit down.'

'Are you sure? I can come back some other time if — '

'No, no, please. It's okay. It was just a . . . a surprise, that's all. I think about

Mike all the time, you know, and for a moment there, when I first came through the door — '

'You thought I was him, didn't you?' he said softly. 'Same build, same colourin'. The other guys used to call us the Bobbsey Twins.'

She laughed. She actually *laughed*. And she couldn't remember the last time she'd done that.

'I'm sorry for the shock,' he said.

'Don't be. It was a nice one. For a second I thought I had him back.'

They made themselves comfortable on the sofa. Jack said, 'Well, how are you? Or is that a dumb question?'

'I'm fine,' she said quickly.

'Really?' he asked, obviously not believing a word of it.

Her shoulders slumped a notch. 'All right,' she replied without criticism, 'it was a dumb question.'

'Then that's another apology I owe you.'

'Mike and I,' she said, 'we were so close. We'd known each other ever since we were kids. Even now I wake up every morning and for a while I think he's still here. Then I remember he isn't and . . . ' She fell silent, then studied him with new interest as something suddenly occurred to her. 'I'm sorry, but I don't remember seeing you at the funeral.'

'I couldn't make the funeral,' he replied. 'The roadside bomb that . . . that took out our APC also took *me* out, for a while.'

'I'm sorry to hear that.'

'Don't be. I was the lucky one. At least I survived. Those other guys . . . ' He broke off for a moment, then said, 'You know, this is crazy.'

'What is?'

'Oh, I had it all planned out, what I was gonna say when I got here. You know, how it was a privilege to serve alongside Mike and what a great guy he was. I meant every word of it, too. But now that I'm actually *here* . . . I don't really think I can tell you anythin' about him that you don't already know.'

'No?'

'No, ma'am. You knew him better than anyone, I reckon. All I have to do is take one look in your eyes to see how much you still love him. A man has to be pretty special to earn the kind of love that lasts like that.'

Her expression soured. 'I think most people would be more inclined to tell me it's about time I accepted that he's gone and moved on with my life.'

'I'm sure they would, ma'am, even though that's a heap easier said than done. Still . . . '

'What? And please, call me Sarah.'

'Well,' he said, a little hesitantly now, 'your eyes tell me just how much Mike meant — *means* — to you. But they tell me somethin' else besides.'

'Which is . . . ?'

'Just how badly losin' him tore you up inside,' he said.

She looked away from him, somehow ashamed that the truth should be so obvious.

'I don't mean to speak out of turn,'

he went on, his tone still gentle. 'But sometimes I think it's better to come right out and say what you mean than straddle the fence.'

'And what *is* it that you mean, exactly?' she asked, looking back at him, but warily now.

'That the one person who'd want you to accept the truth of it and, like you say, move on with your life, is Mike himself. No matter how hard that might be to do.'

Her expression darkened suddenly. 'Did my parents put you up to this?' she asked sharply. 'Was this little pep-talk *their* idea?'

'No ma' — I mean, Sarah.'

'Because I've tried, you know. You wouldn't *believe* how hard I've tried.'

'I think I might,' he said mildly.

'But — '

'Yes?'

'Oh . . . forget it.'

'No, go on. Maybe that's what you need — to talk it out.'

She believed he was probably right

70

about that. 'It's like . . . I don't know, it's like there's a *barrier*. Does that make sense? I *want* to get over losing him, but there's always something holding me back.'

'Which is . . . ?'

Her sigh was eloquent. 'Oh, I don't know. Everything. Guilt, maybe. You know, because it feels like I'm turning my back on him, forgetting he ever existed. But mostly my son.' She eyed him closer. 'Have you met Ryan yet?'

'In passin',' he said. 'He was on his way out when I arrived.'

'I wish there was something I could do,' she said, 'you know, to help him cope. But I suppose he's got to work through it in his own way.'

'Or find someone to give him a hand,' he muttered.

'I've tried that,' she said defensively.

'I didn't say otherwise, ma'am.'

'No, I . . . I suppose not. But I have. And nothing I've done has helped. It's like he blames me for what happened. Not just me — all of us. I don't know

71

what we can do to make him think otherwise. But if I could . . . if only I could . . . *then* I think we could start to heal.'

Tears filled her eyes and she quickly swiped them away.

'I didn't mean to upset you — ' he began.

'You didn't,' she replied, fighting it, pulling herself back together. 'This is pretty much how I am all the time now.'

'Then maybe we ought to do somethin' about that,' he said.

She looked at him. 'Such as?'

But before he could reply Ken and Lynn came back in, Ken carrying a tray with fresh coffee.

'So,' he said briskly, 'tell us some more about that ranch of yours . . . cowboy.'

With a self-conscious grin Jack did just that, and spoke with such obvious love for his home state that it was easy to picture the wild, rugged country in which his family had settled and built their spread.

The next two hours passed more like two minutes, at least to Ken. But eventually Jack checked his wristwatch and said he'd taken enough of their time and should really be making tracks.

'Are you heading back to Texas today?' asked Lynn as they all accompanied him to the door.

'No, ma'am. I've booked a nice little room at the Perkins House, over on Mill Street. Plan to stay over there tonight and be on my way first light tomorrow.'

'Well, why don't you come back later, have supper with us?' asked Lynn.

'Oh, I couldn't — '

'Beats eating alone,' said Ken, warming to the notion. 'And you'd be more than welcome.'

Jack looked at Sarah, his sandy brows arching in question. Shyly, and having no idea why she should feel that way around him, she shrugged. 'Why not? Say about six o'clock?'

'All right,' he said, and grinned again.

'Thank you, folks. I 'preciate it.'

Sarah walked him out to his old firebrick-red Land Cruiser. When they reached the car and were out of earshot of her parents he said, 'I don't have to come for supper if you'd sooner I didn't, you know.'

She frowned at him. 'Why would I want that?'

'Maybe 'cause I spoke out of turn earlier.'

'By telling me that I should go on without Mike, you mean?'

'No ma'am. By tellin' you that as hard as it is to do that, no one would want it *more* than Mike. There's a difference.'

'I only wish it was that easy.'

'Well, nobody said it was gonna be *that*. But sometimes, when a thing's so hard it seems next to impossible . . . ' He shrugged. 'Aw, forget it. Just more of my foolishness.'

'No, go on. Say it, cowboy.'

He looked down at her for a long moment, then said, 'Sometimes you

74

have to find a *reason* to be strong enough to fix things. You got two, I reckon.'

'Oh?'

'Yes'm. Your boy, Ryan. Sounds to me he's runnin' wild, and havin' as hard a time as you at just acceptin' things.'

'That's certainly true enough. And the second reason?'

'What this is doin' to your folks,' he said soberly, remembering the sorrow he'd seen in Ken's eyes, eyes that were still moist from the tears he'd so recently shed. 'You think Mike wants to see you wastin' your life? You think he wants to see Ryan throwin' his away like he is? Think it's any easier on your folks to see what losin' Mike's done to you and the boy?'

She felt herself bristling again. 'You're good at giving advice,' she remarked.

He allowed one broad shoulder to rise and fall. 'Maybe that's because I've had troubles too,' he replied. 'Except that I had the sense to learn from what life taught me.'

'And I haven't?'

'There you go, Sarah, puttin' words in my mouth again. I'm only tryin' to help.'

All at once she sagged and felt as if she were more tired than it was possible to feel. 'I know you mean well,' she sighed. 'But you don't know our situation.'

'Sarah,' he said sadly, 'you don't know *mine*.'

7

Jack climbed into his beat-up Toyota just as a dark cloud passed over the sun, transforming the day. He threw Sarah and her parents a wave and then drove away, telling himself he was seven different kinds of fool to have poked his nose into somebody else's business. Where he came from, that just wasn't done. You could be as neighbourly as you liked, if you were *asked*. But you never poked your nose into another person's affairs without being invited first.

Well, he'd come out here to see Mike's people and pay his respects. He'd done that, best as he'd been able. There was a lot more he'd wanted to say, to Sarah *and* her boy. But somehow the opportunity hadn't presented itself. Maybe tonight, though. And if not, well . . . when he was back home he'd write her a letter or an email and say everything he'd wanted to say in that.

Still, he hated to think of Mike's people being caught up in such an unhappy situation. Mike himself would have felt the same way if the position had been reversed and it was Mike going to visit his, Jack's, folks. He'd have felt obligated to do whatever he could to help, even though he wasn't exactly sure what that was. Instinct told him it was a little straight talking, but that hadn't gone down too well with Sarah.

He was just crossing a seemingly quiet intersection when a bicycle rider suddenly came right out of nowhere on his left. He quickly stamped his foot on the brake, bringing the Land Cruiser to a screeching halt before he could hit the cyclist. Even so, the protesting squeal of his tires threw a scare the size of Texas into the kid on the bike and he lost his footing on one of the pedals, wobbled dangerously and then crashed sideways onto the asphalt, his cell phone leaving his jeans pocket to skitter across the roadway.

Shaken up, Jack got out of the car and stormed across to the boy, who was now climbing back to his feet, his bicycle's wheels spinning with a laddery click-click-click.

'*You!*' said Jack.

Ryan's return glance was baleful. Until he'd recognized Jack he had been a child, shaken by the near miss and afraid of being scolded. The minute he realized who had so nearly knocked him down, however, all the youth in him seemed to vanish, to be replaced by that belligerent, old-before-his-time quality.

'You bonehead!' yelled Ryan.

Jack towered over him, but to give the boy credit, he showed no sign of being intimidated, and absolutely no intention of backing down — and that was pure Mike all the way.

'You could've killed me!' snapped the boy.

'Well, happen you want to live to a ripe old age,' Jack replied testily, 'my advice to you is to *watch where you're goin'!'*

'I *was* watching, thank you very much!'

'Not from where I was sittin', kid.'

'Don't call me kid.'

'It's what you are, isn't it?'

Ignoring him, Ryan turned his attention to his cell, going over and scooping it up before inspecting it for damage. Following him over, Jack took a cursory glance and said, 'It's like you, kid. It'll live to fight another day, I reckon.'

'No thanks to you.'

'Well, I sure hope you're not expecting an apology.'

'I hope *you're* not.'

'That'd be too much from you, I bet,' said Jack. He looked down at the boy, wondering suddenly if he could perhaps turn this chance encounter to his advantage.

'Here,' he said abruptly, and turning, went back to the fallen bicycle and picked it up.

'Hey! What're you doing with my bike? You stealing it or something?'

'Or something,' Jack replied over one shoulder. He carried the machine to his Toyota and lifted it into the back. Then, to Ryan: 'Get in, kid. I'll give you a ride home. Make sure you get there in one piece.'

Ryan snorted. 'Like *you* care.'

'Just get in.'

'What, so you can kidnap me? No way, José.'

Jack sighed. 'Do I *look* like a kidnapper?'

'I don't know. What's a kidnapper look like?'

Jack fought the urge to smile. 'Look, I was a friend of your dad's,' he said, trying to moderate his tone. 'A good friend. I'm hardly likely to do anything to harm his pride and joy.'

'How do I know?'

''cause I just told you,' Jack gritted. 'And where I come from, you can set store by a man's word.'

For a moment the boy looked as if he

were going to refuse the offer. Then, perhaps realizing he still had a fair piece to go before he reached his grandparents' place, and it was beginning to look increasingly like rain, he grudgingly climbed in beside Jack.

'You talk funny,' he said.

'That's strange,' said Jack. 'If you was in *my* neck of the woods, I 'spect we'd say the same about *you*.'

He started the engine and drove off.

'My folks live thataway,' said Ryan, hooking a thumb back in the opposite direction.

'I know. We'll get there directly. But first, I want a few words with you, boy.'

'Do you, now?'

'You know somethin', son?'

'I'm not your son!'

'Just a figure of speech . . . *son*. But it strikes me you've got quite a chip on your shoulder.'

'What's that to do with you?'

'Nothin'. But it has a whole lot to do with your mother — an' your dad.'

'You leave my dad out of this,'

muttered the boy.

'All right. But what I'm about to say about your mother applies equally well to your dad, Ryan. She hates to see you like this. She'd sooner you opened up and told her how you felt — '

'She *knows* how I feel.'

'No she doesn't. She can guess well enough. But *know?* No way, son — I'm sorry; *Ryan*. She can't even *begin* to understand how you feel, unless you tell her. And that particular trail runs both ways. You might think you've got *her* all figured out, but you haven't.'

Ryan subjected Jack's profile to his fiercest glare. 'And what would you know about it? I didn't even know you before today.'

'I know about loss, boy. More'n you might realize. And I know that it's a hard thing to accept, 'specially when you're just a kid. You keep all that stuff bottled up and . . . well, let's jus' say it reminds me of an old-timer I knew back when I was about your age. Feller named Bud Owen.'

He fell silent and appeared to be concentrating more on driving them through Milford's vast suburban sprawl. But that was just an act. He'd grown up on a ranch, around stubborn cattle and horses that rarely if ever wanted to be broken to the saddle. In cases like that, it was always best to let such ornery critters come to you.

After another moment Ryan said, almost against his will, 'What about this Owen character?'

Jack drew a breath. 'Well, he was out chasing up strays one day when he got bit by a snake. A coral snake, as I recall: here, on the back of his right hand. It was just an itty-bitty snake, not much longer or thicker'n a bootlace. And because of that, ol' Bud didn't think there was anythin' to worry about. I mean, that snake, he was just a little strip of nothin', right?

'So Bud wrapped his hand with his neckerchief and figured it would heal all by itself. But it didn't. When he woke up next mornin' his hand was about twice its normal size, skin stretched tight as a drum and so tender to the touch that he couldn't use it for nothin' at all, couldn't even flex his fingers. And the colour!' He shuddered. 'You know what an eggplant is, son?'

'Sure.'

'Well, Bud's skin was about the same colour, a real dark kind of purple, kind of shiny, too.'

He fell silent again, waited . . . waited . . .

'What happened to him?' the boy asked at length.

Jack threw a look at him. 'Well, he went to see a doctor, but the doctor said he'd left it too late. If Bud had come to him sooner instead of jus' leavin' it, things wouldn't have gotten so bad for him. As it was, he'd allowed that wound to fester, and in festerin' it filled up with all kinds of poison, see. So he sent Bud to the hospital with the recommendation that they amputate before the poison could spread.'

Another long pause. Finally the boy

said reluctantly, 'And did they?'

'No. Surgeon at the hospital took a good long look at it and decided they could maybe fix him up a better way. See, the surgeon knew that wound wasn't ever gonna get any better unless they drained all the poison out of it first, so that's what they did. They drained it, cleaned it up and it got better. No need to amputate after all.'

Without looking at the boy he continued, 'It's the same with you, Ryan. Losin' your dad . . . in its way that was like a wound, too. The smart thing would have been to take all that sadness and confusion and hurt and let it all out. But who feels smart when they're hurtin' so bad? No one.'

The boy considered that for a while, then said, 'So you're saying I should have told my mom how I felt about . . . about losing my dad.'

'Uh-huh. You can't keep stuff like that bottled up, Ryan, else it turns bad.'

'So what do I do?' asked the boy. 'To drain it, I mean?'

'*Share* it,' said Jack. 'Just talk, and let someone else listen. Someone you trust, who's willing to hear you out. You never know, takin' them feelin's and puttin' 'em into words might just help you understand 'em better. But I'll promise you this, son. Things won't get any better as long as you let 'em keep festerin'.'

'Well, I'm doing fine just as I am, thank you very much,' said Ryan.

'Not from where I'm sittin'.'

'No?'

'No, sir. From where I'm sittin' all I see's a kid who thinks the world owes him a favour; a kid who treats the people who love him the most just about as bad as he can.'

Ryan shrugged uncomfortably. 'You know it all, don't you?'

'Nope. But I know *this* much, son.'

'Don't — '

'I know you hate the world for takin' your daddy away, and I know you hate your folks — leastways you *think* you hate them — for allowin' it to happen.

But what say did they have in it? Do you think they'd have let it happen if there was any way they could have avoided it? When was the last time you thought about anyone other than yourself, Ryan? Take a look at your mom, or your grandparents . . . don't you see that losing your dad broke *their* hearts as well?'

'It's not the same,' said Ryan truculently.

'The hell it's not,' Jack replied. 'It's all a question of . . . degree. Your folks are older than you are, so maybe that's why they've handled it better. But that's my advice, son, for what it's worth. Get all that bad stuff out of your system, and then try thinkin' about someone *else* for a change.'

'Where the hell do you get off, telling me what to do?' demanded the boy.

'First place, quit that cussin'.'

'What, 'hell'? You said it, just now.'

'That's different. I'm a grown-up. You're only sayin' it 'cause you think it makes you sound grown-up as well, but you're wrong — it don't.'

'Doesn't,' Ryan smirked. 'How can you tell me how to talk when you don't even know how to talk yourself?'

Without warning Jack pulled over to the side of the road and braked, then killed the engine. A cool wind had sprung up, pushing in more clouds the colour of bruises that threatened a bad storm ahead. Glancing around, Ryan was startled to discover that they were at the very top of the street where he lived.

'You know what, boy?' said Jack. 'Other folks might walk soft around you because of that big bad attitude of yourn, but it don't work with me. You're all hat and no cattle, like we say back home. But I know why you act the way you do and say the things you say. You're hurtin', and you don't want the rest of the world to see it. So you put on a front and that's how you get through each day.'

'You got a problem with that?' growled the boy.

'No, sir. But where I *do* have a problem is when *your* way of gettin' through the day hurts the people around you, and stops them from getting through *their* day. And it *does*, Ryan. You want to open your eyes and really see what you're lookin' at, boy. A mother who's just about worn to a frazzle and two grandparents that ain't much better. You've worn 'em down, Ryan. *You*.'

'Thanks. That makes me feel so much better.'

'Well, don't fret, kid. That's the bad news. Now here's the good. It's not too late to turn things around and repair all the damage.'

'And how do I do that?'

'There's no trick to it. You just start to put other folks before yourself. You ought to try it sometime. Never know, it might even get to become a habit.'

Jack got out of the Toyota and dragged Ryan's bike out of the back. 'I'll leave you to go the rest of the way by yourself,' he said. 'No need for your folks to know we had this little conversation.'

Ryan climbed out, curiously reluctant to leave the big Texan's company, and took the bike. He seemed subdued, almost in a state of mild shock. Jack hoped it meant that some of what he'd said had hit home. He had a feeling things would be better for Mike's folks if it did.

'I'll see you later, Ryan,' he said. The boy looked a question at him and he explained, 'Your folks've invited me to supper.'

'Oh.'

'I'll see you about six,' said Jack.

He climbed back into the Toyota and drove away.

Meanwhile, the storm clouds continued to gather.

8

Ryan had heard that old saying about the truth hurting many times in the past, but it was only as he went into his bedroom and slammed the door hard behind him that he realized just how true it was. He *had* been a pain in the butt for his folks. He saw that now — had probably seen it all along, but just didn't want to admit it. At just the time when he should have been thinking about his mom and grandparents, he'd chosen to think only about himself, and the crazy thing was that in doing that he hadn't made himself feel one iota better.

He remembered all the times he'd secretly felt sorry for treating his folks the way he did; the way he'd always quickly stifled those feelings, considering them signs of weakness, and tried to convince himself that he was right and they were wrong — that somehow he was the only one who really mattered.

Now he felt like a spoilt little brat. And he *was*. A stupid, immature, mixed-up, spiteful little brat.

But knowing that didn't make the truth any easier to bear.

He flicked on the CD player at full volume, threw himself onto his bed and stared up at the ceiling. He thought of his mother — how he should have been there for her when his dad died, and become the man of the house. But he hadn't done anything except make everything so much worse for her.

Did he *really* think she'd lost his dad's Silver Star on purpose? Of course not. He'd just wanted to feel that she was somehow adding insult to injury, like *he* was the victim in all of this.

And Gramps . . . for the first time he thought of just how difficult it must have been for Gramps to have to tell a ten-year-old kid such bad news. They'd always been close, so it must have been terrible for him. But once again, good old Ryan hadn't done anything but make things even harder for him.

Emotion tightened his throat, but he felt somehow unable to let it out. Still, he felt very strongly in that moment that his folks must despise him for having made their lives hell.

They'd be better off without him.

He saw that clearly now, and saw equally clearly exactly what he would do about it.

He got up, went to his wardrobe and took out an old orange canvas backpack. Then, as quickly as he could, he stuffed a few changes of clothes into it. He was going to get out of his mom's life, his grandparents' lives, and when he was gone he'd be one less problem for them to have to handle.

He also knew exactly where he was going to go.

But he needed supplies: food, something to drink. Just enough to hold him until he could decide on his next move. And for that he needed money.

Even as he thought it his blue eyes

— a child's eyes now, no longer those of someone much older and so seemingly cynical — came to rest upon the small red box containing the Silver Star. Gramps must have put it back on the chest of drawers after the Texan returned it.

He snatched up the box. On the bottom there was a sticker. It read Mrs. Catt's Curiosities and gave an address on Main. That must have been where Gramps bought it.

He stuffed the box in his pocket and then went to the window. There he carefully lowered his backpack to the grass outside, then followed it out, all the time glancing around, determined that no one should see him leave.

He grabbed up the backpack, then trotted around the side of the house to his bike. He threw the backpack up across his shoulders and snugged it tight, then mounted the bike . . . and quickly pedalled away.

★   ★   ★

Mrs. Catt was fussing at her cluttered shelves with a gaily coloured feather duster when she heard the store door open behind her. She turned just as a blond-haired boy with blue eyes and a very serious expression came inside, holding a small red box in one hand.

Mrs. Catt immediately put on her glasses . . . but only so that she could regard the boy expectantly from *above* their bejewelled frame. 'Good afternoon,' she said.

The boy shrugged awkwardly, the movement shifting the backpack he wore. 'I want to get a refund,' he said.

'Do you, now?'

'It's on this medal. It's the Silver Star.'

'I know,' she replied, going around to the business side of her glass counter. 'I only sold it this morning.'

'Yeah, to my gramps. Uh, my grandfather.'

Mrs. Catt cocked her head at the boy. 'Is there something wrong with it?' she asked.

'No.'

'Then why do you want a refund?'

The boy pursed his lips. 'I don't want it.'

'He bought it for *you*, is that what you're telling me?'

'Uh-huh.'

'Then it was your father who . . . ?'

'We lost his Silver Star. Gramps thought I'd like another one. I don't.'

'So you want your money back?'

'Uh-huh.'

'Well, I'm sorry to disappoint you, young man, but I can only give you store credit.'

Ryan's expression slackened. '*What?*'

'That's my policy, I'm afraid,' said Mrs. Catt. 'If there was something wrong with it, I'd cheerfully give you your money back.'

'Well, can't you just . . . pretend? Just this once?'

She offered him an indulgent smile. 'If I did it for you, I'd have to do it for everyone, wouldn't I?'

'I wouldn't tell.'

'I'm sure you wouldn't. But do you know something? I really think you'd be happier if you were to *keep* that medal. It might not be the one you lost, but . . . well, who's to say it isn't? Besides, it's what it represents that matters.' She looked him straight in the face and said meaningfully, 'An acknowledgement of what your dad gave . . . what he sacrificed . . . for the country he loved.'

It was so close to what Gramps had told him earlier that day, almost word for word, that he gawped at her.

'Did my gramps tell you that?' he asked.

'No.'

'Then why did you say it?'

'Because it's *true*,' she replied simply. 'Now, will it be store credit, young man? Or do you want to give that medal a chance to grow on you?'

He looked down at the box, thinking that this had been a crazy day and that it had just gotten a little crazier.

'I'll give it a chance,' he said, then turned and left.

* * *

It had just started raining lightly when Jack arrived at the Weavers' a little before six o'clock that evening. The front door of the ranch-style house opened even before he was halfway up the path, a bottle of wine in one hand and two bunches of flowers, one for Sarah, one for Lynn, in the other. And when Sarah came outside and hurried towards him, he took one look at her face and knew that something was wrong.

'What is it?' he asked.

Sarah answered the question with one of her own as they hurried back to the house side by side. 'You didn't see Ryan anywhere, did you? As you drove in?'

'No.'

The news seemed to deflate her.

'What's happened?' he asked, aware that Ken and Lynn were waiting anxiously in the hallway.

'He's run away,' she said.

'What?'

'He spent all afternoon in his room, playing music,' she said as they entered the house and she closed the door behind them. 'At least that's what we thought. Then, about four o'clock, I went to have a word with him and got no answer. I went in and found the room empty.' Her teal-blue eyes were pools of despair as she added tremulously, 'His backpack's gone, and so are some of his clothes.'

Before he could stop himself Jack muttered, 'Damn.'

She frowned up at him. 'What is it?' she asked.

His expression was sheepish as he looked from Sarah's parents to Sarah herself. 'I ran into him this afternoon,' he said, adding mentally, *Almost literally.* 'We had some words.'

'What do you mean?'

'I guess I told him a few home truths,' he said.

Ken stepped forward. 'You *what?*'

'I didn't mean for this to happen,'

he continued. 'I just thought that maybe — ' He bit off suddenly. Sarah didn't want to hear his feeble attempt at an apology, not right now. All she wanted now was her boy back.

'Any idea where he might've gone?' he asked.

'No.'

'Does he have any favourite haunts?'

'I don't know.'

'Arcades? The local McDonald's?'

'I don't know,' she repeated helplessly. 'If he did, he certainly never mentioned them.'

'How about a friend?' Jack pursued. 'Does he have a best friend? Someone who'd put him up for the night — or know where he might've gone?'

'No.'

'Have you tried callin' him on his cell?'

Her look was withering. That was the first thing she'd done. 'He's just not answering.'

'Then maybe we ought to call the police.'

Sarah looked aghast. 'If I do that he'll *never* forgive me.' She thought briefly, then said, 'But I'm going to call the bus station again, and see if anyone answering Ryan's description has shown there up yet.'

'What did you say to him, Jack?' asked Lynn, watching as he set the wine and flowers down on the dining table. 'What did you say to upset him?'

'Nothin' that was meant to make him run away,' he replied honestly. Then, even as Sarah picked up the phone: 'It's okay, Sarah. We'll round him up.'

'Round him — !' She snorted, slamming the handset down again. 'He's not one of the cattle on your precious ranch, Jack! He's a twelve-year-old boy, dammit!'

He turned away from her, thinking, *trying* to think. The burden of responsibility weighed heavily on him. He didn't think he'd said anything to make the boy react this way. If he'd thought that for just one moment . . .

He turned back to Sarah and her

parents. 'Give me his cell phone number,' he snapped.

'He won't answer,' said Lynn.

'That's not why I want it,' he replied, and pulled out his own mobile phone. 'Could be we can find out where he is through his phone.'

'It's not registered with any tracking company,' said Sarah.

'For what I've got in mind, it doesn't have to be,' he replied. He went through his contacts, found the number he wanted and hit OK with one thumb. While it rang he said, 'Couple fellers I knew in the Ivy worked in communications. When they got out they set 'emselves up in the technology business. They should be able to locate Ryan's phone to within a few yards.'

'Can they *do* that?' asked Ken. 'I mean, is it legal?'

'I don't know about that,' Jack replied, 'but I'd say in this case the end justifies the means, wouldn't you?' Then, into the phone: 'Sam? It's Jack Donovan . . . Yeah, fine. Listen, I need a fix on someone's cell phone. Can you . . . ? It's a boy. Mike Nelson's boy. He's gone missin'.'

He looked at Sarah, who had taken out her own cell, located Ryan's number and now held it up so that Jack could read it. He passed the number along to his former army buddy and then waited a few tense moments.

After what seemed like forever he murmured some figures, gestured for Ken to write them down and said, 'Thanks, Sam. That's one I owe you.'

As he ended the call and shoved the phone back into his jeans pocket, Ken asked him, 'What have I just written down?'

'The latitude and longitude of Ryan's phone, as of about thirty seconds ago,' Jack replied. 'Have you got a local map, Mr. Weaver?'

'Sure.'

Ken fetched it, spread it out on the dining table and they all gathered around while Jack pored over it. After a couple of minutes he tapped a spot and said, 'I make it right about . . . *here*.'

Lynn frowned. 'That's up in the woods about three miles northwest of here.'

'Well, that's where we'll find him — or his phone.'

'But what's he doing way up there?'

'When I find him,' said Jack, heading for the door, 'I'll ask him.'

'Wait a minute,' said Sarah, hurrying to match his long strides. 'I'm coming with you.'

It was on the tip of his tongue to tell her to stay behind and sit tight, but he knew he had no right to do that. Sarah was Ryan's mother. When they found him — he refused to think in terms of *if* — then he might appreciate a familiar face.

'Grab a jacket,' he said, just as the first rumble of thunder rolled across the sky. 'It's gonna get rough out there.'

9

Ryan peered up through the canopy of interlaced branches that spanned the shallow stream and dyed this part of the forest a dull olive green, and thought that maybe this hadn't been such a good idea after all.

He had no money, and consequently no supplies. He was hungry, he was thirsty and he was . . . it hurt to admit it, but it could hardly be denied: he was *scared*.

Thunder rumbled across the lowering sky. He felt it vibrate in his teeth, in his bones. Rain set up a constant hiss as it tapped insistently against leaves that wilted under the onslaught. He watched it stitch the surface of the stream and shivered. Night was coming early. And with the night the cave, the one place he had always figured he knew peace of mind, was beginning to fill up with

shadows and look decidedly threatening.

I've got to spend the night here, he
told himself. *All alone, in the pitch
black. I didn't even think to fetch a
flashlight.*

Before the storm started he'd been
fine. He'd reckoned he could make
himself reasonably comfortable tonight
and then tomorrow he'd go foraging
and maybe live off nuts and berries for
a while, until he decided his next move.

But then the sky had darkened and
he'd started to become aware of
strange, inexplicable noises drifting to
him from the deepest woods.

He'd started thinking about all those
tracks he'd seen on his countless
previous trips up here, of white-tail deer
and coyotes, but more than that he
thought about all the stories he'd heard
about these same wooded slopes
harbouring black and brown bears, red
and gray wolves, bobcats and lynxes
and wolverines.

Was that true, or had he just read it

somewhere? Maybe they didn't inhabit this part of the country at all. After all, he'd never found their tracks —

Something out in the darkness snapped with a sound like a gunshot and he hastily withdrew his head and backed deeper into the cave.

I'm scared, he thought miserably.

Then he thought of the medal.

Okay, so it probably wasn't *the* Silver Star, the one that had belonged to his dad. But what was it that was engraved on the reverse side? FOR GALLANTRY IN ACTION. Okay, so he was in action now — kind of — and he was going to be as gallant as his dad had been.

He reached into his pocket for the medal box, knowing it would give him the courage to get through the night, and stiffened in alarm when he couldn't find it.

Turning panicky now, he quickly checked his other pockets, the pockets in his jacket. He'd had it when he'd left Mrs. Catt's store, he *knew* he had. Had he put it in his backpack?

He grabbed the pack, took it to the cave entrance to make the most of the quick-fading light and rummaged through it but came up empty.

Where the heck is it?

He must've lost it somehow.

How dumb can you get? he demanded of himself. *Now you don't even —*

Lightning flared across the sky, lighting the forest for just a moment, and hard on its heels came the loudest clash of thunder so far. Ryan almost jumped out of his skin — then froze.

For in that single, split-second flare of lightning he could have sworn . . . he could have *sworn* . . .

He could have sworn he saw something watching him from the opposite bank.

Something large and monstrous.

* * *

Jack followed the track until it finally petered out, then pulled the Land Cruiser off into tall grass and killed the engine and windshield wipers. 'Stay here,' he said, snatching up Ken's map and reaching into the jockey box for a long waterproof flashlight. 'I won't come back without him, I promise.'

It was the first words either of them had spoken since they left the house. There was nothing else to say. Jack felt he was very much the villain in all of this, and though he didn't necessarily see it that way himself, he *did* feel responsible for what had happened. With hindsight he allowed that he probably could have made his point in a less heavy-handed fashion. But how was he to know that Ryan would take it into his head to leave home as a consequence?

As he climbed out of the Toyota he was reminded of that old saw about the road to hell being paved with good intentions. *Looks like it's true after all*, he thought ruefully. Which meant that the very least he could do now was bring Ryan back home, even if that in turn meant searching every square inch of this wilderness to do so.

'I'm coming with you,' said Sarah. Her words were almost lost beneath the insistent drumming of rain against the hood of the car.

'You'll get soaked,' he said. 'We're in for a real gully-washer.'

'You think I care about that?'

He almost flinched at the hostility in her tone and said mildly, 'I guess not.'

They set off side by side into the forest, Jack casting the flashlight beam out ahead of them. The rain was almost torrential now, though the interlaced tree branches kept the worst of it off. Even so, the ground underfoot was rapidly turning slippery, and they were halfway up a grassy rise when Jack suddenly lost his footing and slipped, and Sarah quickly reached out to catch his arm and steady him.

'You okay?' she asked.

He nodded, to her surprise a little shaken by the near-fall.

'Sure *you* don't want to wait behind?' she added. 'At this rate I can probably make better time by myself — '

He looked at her with such a strange expression on his face that she instantly regretted the sarcasm.

'I'm comin',' he said, and started back up the slope. 'You might just need me to navigate, don't forget.'

That brought a new concern to her mind. 'You're right,' she breathed in sudden despair. 'We don't have a compass!'

'We don't need one,' he told her, running the flashlight beam across the surrounding trees.

'Well, you certainly can't navigate by the stars,' she said testily. 'Not unless you can see through all that cloud.'

'I don't have to,' he replied. 'These trees'll tell us all we need to know.'

'What do you mean?'

He gestured with the flashlight. 'Trees always have fewer branches on their north side. And that's the side moss prefers to grow on.'

'Are you kidding me?'

'No, ma'am. Here, see? And here on

this far side . . . that there's an anthill — and ants always like to build their hills on the south side.'

'You really *are* a backwoodsman, aren't you?'

'Where I come from this kinda thing's a way of life.'

'So long as it helps me find Ryan.'

He took her by one arm. 'If he's here for the findin',' he assured her, 'we'll find him.'

She looked up into his face, into the pools of shadow that had become his eyes, at the firm, determined jut of his jaw, and believed him.

Around them the woods were dark and a fine mist was rising up off the ground as the temperature continued to plunge. They pushed on, trending first one way, then another, Jack always keeping an eye on his surroundings to make sure they were moving in the right direction.

After a while he stopped and checked the now-soggy map again. Unless he missed his guess, they were now within a hoot and a holler of Ryan's last known position. That being the case, he passed the flashlight to Sarah and then cupped his hands around his mouth.

'*Ryan? Ryan! It's okay, son, we've come to take you home!*'

The only reply was an ominous growl of thunder.

'*RYAN!*'

Sarah walked on a few paces, until she reached a stream — moving fast now, as it swelled with rainwater — set between steep, shale-covered banks. Jack followed her, stuffing the map away. Lightning flashed through the spider's web of interlaced branches above them, throwing charcoal-gray shadows across spilled boulders covered in moss that looked more like green velvet.

'*RYAN!*'

Jack's voice was soaked up by the storm.

'What if he's moved on?' Sarah asked, despair once again threatening to overwhelm her. 'What if your army friends were wrong?'

He turned to reply and as he did so he froze. 'They weren't,' he said.

She looked at him, eyelids flickering in the downpour. 'How can you be so sure?'

Instead of answering her he crossed to an area of shale beside the stream, bent and picked something up. When he held it out to her she gasped.

'That's the box the medal came in!'

Jack checked inside. 'Medal's still inside, too.'

'He probably threw it away,' she said.

'Whether he threw it away or jus' plain lost it, it proves he was around here someplace — and that he might still be.'

'*RYAN!*'

This time it was Sarah's voice that echoed through the seemingly empty forest.

Jack bent at the waist and said, 'Throw some of that light this way.'

She did so. He studied the ground

intently. At length he said, 'There! See here, in the soft earth? Tire tracks.' He lifted one brawny arm to point. 'He went that way.'

'Then so do we,' she said.

★ ★ ★

Ryan stared out into the darkness, wondering what it was that he'd seen. He tried to play that now-you-see-it, now-you-don't image back through his mind, but it had happened so fast —

It wasn't anything that walked on four legs, that much was sure. Whatever was on the other side of the stream had been standing upright. A man? Or something *like* a man?

A bear?

A bigfoot?

Was there even any such *thing* as a bigfoot?

He really didn't want to find out.

In his panic, however, he didn't even consider the possibility that he had

116

simply misidentified the twisted remnants of a dead tree.

Heart racing now, he backed deeper into the cave, not daring to take his eyes off that patch of inky blackness on the far side of the stream. When a moment later thunder and lightning coincided, he got another far-from-good look at the spot where he'd seen his 'monster', only now —

Now the monster was gone.

It had moved.

Crossed the stream? he wondered.

Was it coming for him even now, as the forest was plunged back into darkness?

Fumbling, he reached through the blackness for his bike, figuring to lay it across the opening of the cave almost like a trap. That way, if anything tried to get at him it would trip on the bike first and forewarn him, give him a chance to get past it — whatever *it* was — and run for his life —

In a brief lull in the downpour he caught a sound, like . . . like shale sliding across shale . . .

It was on this side of the stream, then.

It really *was* coming to get him.

In that moment a curious calm settled across him. All right — let it come. His dad had been Mike Nelson, and he'd been awarded a Silver Star for gallantry. That bear, or bigfoot or whatever it was . . . it wouldn't find him any less gallant, when it came to it.

Setting the bike to one side, he planted himself there in the centre of the cave, waiting for it to show itself, and not knowing what he would do when it did — only that he would fight it with all the strength he had in him.

Again, that sound of shale sliding across shale.

Thunder boomed overhead and buzzed in his ears.

Come on, he thought, almost unable to bear the tension, *come on* . . .

And then —

'Ryan! Ryan, where are you?'

He swayed a little, disbelief making

him feel almost lightheaded. Was that his *mom?* Out there, in the storm?

He hurried to the cave mouth just as lightning burst across the heavens above the trees, and threw shadows like a fisherman's net over the racing stream and the steep, shaly bank and —

— and —

'MOM!?'

Sarah, no more than thirty feet away, turned at the sound of his voice. Ryan flinched and squinted as he found himself pinned by the beam of a flashlight.

'Ryan!'

The boy didn't think he'd ever been so glad to see his mother in his life.

10

Jack hung back a moment while Sarah and Ryan hugged, and then Sarah did all the things moms always did at times like that — hold their boy at arm's length and check him for injuries, or malnutrition; whether he'd grown another inch since she last saw him, or just to convince herself that her baby really was here in her arms and he really was okay.

Then Jack climbed up the slope and into the cave, and by flashlight he and the boy exchanged a long, silent look. For once there was no animosity in Ryan's expression — only relief.

Behind Jack, lightning stilt-walked across the turbulent sky. 'Scared, Ryan?' the Texan asked softly.

Ryan's jaw firmed up and he said defiantly, 'No.'

Jack acted as if he hadn't heard him.

'Scared, Ryan?' he asked again.

And this time Ryan dropped his tough-guy act and said, 'Yes.'

To his surprise, Jack grinned at him. 'Congratulations, son,' he said. 'It takes a real man to admit when he's scared.' And to Sarah he said, 'You better call your folks and tell 'em Ryan's okay.'

She tried, but couldn't get a signal.

'This storm's playin' havoc with everything',' Jack opined, glancing out at the sky, across which low, dark clouds continued to scud. 'Told you it was gonna be a gully-washer.'

Ryan smirked, happy now that he had his mom there, he had the big Texan, and he had light to chase away the darkness. 'You sure do talk funny,' he said.

'You mind your manners,' chided Sarah. 'He talks like a *cowboy.*'

'Well, no matter how I talk,' said Jack, 'we're gonna be here a while. Might as well make ourselves comfortable.'

He eased himself down into a sitting

position and Sarah and her son followed suit.

For a while they just sat in silence. Then Sarah said to Ryan, 'You know, you had us scared half to death.'

Ryan cast his eyes groundward. 'I'm sorry. I just thought . . . you know . . . you'd be better off without me.'

'Whatever gave you that idea?' asked Sarah, casting a baleful look at Jack.

Ryan caught it and said, 'Not *him*. It was my idea. All he did was tell me what a jerk I am.'

'What a jerk you *were*,' muttered Jack. 'Seems to me you've changed considerable since we had our little talk — an' for the better.'

Sarah was quiet for a while. At last she said, 'I'm sorry, cowboy.'

'Forget it,' he replied shortly. 'Oh, by the way, Ryan — you dropped somethin' on your way up here.'

He held out the medal box, and was gratified when he saw how eagerly the boy almost snatched it from him.

'Thought I'd lost it,' said the boy.

'Then you see just how easy it really *is* to lose things,' his mother pointed out.

Ryan nodded shamefacedly.

She looked at the medal and inevitably it brought back memories of Mike, and a reminder that he was never going to come back.

'Jack,' she said uncertainly.

'Yes'm?'

'Were you . . . were you with Mike?' she asked softly, and with a swallow finished, ' . . . at the end?'

'Yes, ma'am, I was,' he replied quietly. 'An' that's partly why I came to see you both. I shared those last moments with him — held his hand and told him everything was gonna be okay, even though we both knew it wasn't. And I wanted you to know that I never knew a braver or more decent man. You know when they say, 'He died doing what he believed in'? Well, Mike did. He believed absolutely in why we were there, and what we were tryin' to achieve. If he had to pay the ultimate price for that . . . well, I guess he'd resigned himself to the fact that it was a price worth payin'.'

Sarah's eyes filled with tears. 'There's something . . . maybe I shouldn't ask. Maybe I'd be better off not knowing, but . . . ' With a supreme effort, she steeled herself and said, almost in a whisper, 'Did he suffer?'

'You want the truth?' he replied.

'Of course.'

'The truth is he never really knew what hit him. It was a day like any other. We were doing our job and it just . . . I don't know . . . *happened*. When the dust cleared I was laying there on my belly and my ears were ringin' — no, not ringin', more like whinin' . . . and I literally didn't know who I was or where I was or what was happenin' around me. But there was a part of me . . . a part of my mind that was like . . . *separate* . . . from every-thin' else, and it was in there that I started to put everythin' together.'

The sounds of the storm seemed to

fade into the background as mother and son hung on his every word.

'I managed to push myself up onto and crawl over to Mike. He was on his back, starin' up at the sky, and there was an expression on his face . . . it was almost . . . I don't know. *Serene?* Like he knew what was gonna happen and he wasn't afraid to face it.'

'Could he speak?' asked Ryan, his voice hushed.

'No.'

'Then how do you know he thought it was a price worth paying?' the boy asked with just a touch of his old belligerence.

'Because he smiled at me,' Jack replied simply. 'Hear that? He smiled at me and . . . and kind of nodded. As if he was tryin' to tell me it was okay, you know? Like, it had happened, and there was nothin' we could do to make it *un*-happen.'

He shifted a little so that he could face both of them. 'Don't get me wrong, now. He didn't want to leave you guys. I could see that in his eyes. I looked him in the eye and I saw all the regret there, plain as could be — the regret any man'd feel if he knew he was never gonna see the wife and son he loved so much ever again.'

Ryan snorted. 'You know something?' he said. 'You're full of it, cowboy.'

'Ryan!'

'You are,' Ryan continued. 'You're only telling us what you think we want to hear.'

'I'm not, son.'

'Don't call me that! I'm not your son!'

'I'm sorry.'

'Well don't say it around me ever again!' snapped Ryan, still trying instinctively to mask his true feelings. 'You don't know anything about me! You don't know anything about what it means to lose anyone!'

Jack sat forward suddenly, and the movement was so quick that Ryan actually flinched away from him. 'No?' asked Jack. 'I'll tell you all about loss,

Ryan. I went to Helmand with fifty other guys, and the Taliban whittled 'em down, day after day, and there wasn't a thing I could do to stop it.

'Imagine that for a moment, boy. Imagine all the kids you go to school with, and never knowin' if the kids you're talking to this mornin'll still be around this afternoon. Whether or not *you'll* still be around.'

'All right, Jack . . . ' began Sarah.

But Jack ignored her, and fixing Ryan with a hard look, knowing there was still a little work to be done on the boy, said, 'You want to know what *I* know about loss, boy?'

He reached down and rapped his knuckles against his right leg, just below the knee.

His leg made a hard, unyielding sound.

Sarah stared at him, realizing for the first time just what the bomb that had killed Mike had done to Jack — why he had slipped on the way up here, and why he had looked at her the way he did when she'd made that comment about making better time without him.

He saw it in her face and nodded. 'Yup. Lost my leg just below the knee and in the process kissed goodbye to any plans I had about takin' over the family business. But then you know what happened? I realized that no matter how sorry everyone was about my loss, there was only one person who could really do anythin' about it. *Me.* So I did everythin' they told me to do and I did it for one simple reason — because God or Fate or whatever you want to call it, had given me a chance it didn't give to your dad.'

He broke off abruptly, suddenly filled with emotion, and he looked off into the wild night and thought about everything that his decision had cost him.

After a moment he said, 'Listen to me, son — sorry, *Ryan*. And this goes for you, too, Sarah. You've both been given a gift that was taken away from Mike. Don't throw it away by livin' in the past, or tryin' to convince yourself that the world owes you a livin'. Take what you've got and live it the best way you can, as a tribute to Mike . . . to make up for the life *he* never *got* to live.'

While they pondered that, thunder continued to roll ominously overhead. Jack took another look around and said, 'Give your phone another try, Sarah. Your folks must be half out of their minds.'

Chastened, she tried again, but still the storm was playing havoc with the signal. Then, right out of the blue, Ryan said, 'I've got it!'

Sarah and Jack gathered around him while he speed-dialled his grandfather's number on his own cell and waited. A moment later he said, 'Gramps! It's me! . . . yeah, I'm fine. Mom and the cowboy're are here, too. Yeah . . . yeah, we're all safe . . . we got shelter and we're gonna hole-up here until the . . . hello? Gramps?'

He looked up at Sarah. 'I think the

signal cut out again — ' But then his face brightened. 'Gramps? Yeah, I'm still here. Listen, we're gonna sit the storm out up here . . . However long it takes, I guess . . . Sure, we'll be fine.'

There was another pause, and then Ryan moved away from his mother and Jack, and lowering his voice a little said, 'Hey, Gramps? I love you.'

Sarah looked up at Jack, her eyes suddenly brimming with tears. Jack looked down at her and in that moment was surprised by just how much he wanted to draw her to him and hold her close. Maybe he was just caught up in the moment — but he didn't think so.

Still, it wouldn't be right to do that. She was — *had* been — the wife of his closest friend. She was still hurting, still vulnerable. If ever the time came when she felt it was right to move on and give her emotions to another man, to *him*, maybe, even though he'd lost a leg . . . then that would be her choice, and he would do nothing to rush her.

So all he did was smile back at her

130

and say, 'You got a fine boy there, Mrs. Nelson. And as proud as you are of him right this minute, I bet you're nowhere near as proud as his father.'

'Cowboy,' she replied in a tremulous whisper, 'I do believe you're right.'

* * *

Jack's Land Cruiser pulled up a little after midnight, and by the time Sarah, Jack and Ryan were walking up the path toward the house, Ken and Lynn were already at the door, anxious to greet them after their adventure.

'Home is the hero,' called Jack, putting his hands on Ryan's shoulders and propelling him toward his grandparents.

'And he *has* been a hero, too,' added Sarah. 'It was his private cave where we sheltered. And he was the one who managed to get a signal so that we could tell you we were safe.'

Ryan shrugged and began to blush, but when Ken and Lynn both hugged

131

him, he made no attempt to pull away from them. Indeed, he hugged them right back.

'Come in and tell us all about it,' said Lynn. 'You three must be starving!'

'I could certainly handle a small stack of pancakes about now,' grinned Jack. 'So long as it's not *too* small.'

All in all, it was quite a night for the family. But it was just that — a family affair. And soon, albeit regretfully, Jack rose and said his goodbyes.

Sarah and Ryan saw him out to his car, where Jack and Ryan enjoyed a solemn handshake — until Jack yanked the boy forward into his arms and gave him a squeeze that knocked the air out of him, and which the boy enjoyed no end.

Then Jack turned to face Sarah, and as she looked up at him a hint of colour appeared on her cheeks.

'Will you ever come back this way, Jack?' she asked, suddenly realizing how devastated she would be if she never saw him again.

'I reckon,' he replied. 'But I think I can go one better than that.'

'Oh?'

'Well, it's like I told your folks yesterday, Sarah. Where I come from it's wide-open country. There's good, clean air, and plenty room for a woman and her boy to stretch . . . and maybe start over afresh. We got horses and cattle and rodeos and all kinds of stuff. Be nice if you two'd come out and visit me, sometime. Sometime *soon*.'

Ryan's eyes saucered. 'Oh, man! Could we, Mom?'

Sarah looked up at Jack. 'I'm not sure . . . '

'That's all right,' he said softly. 'I know it's difficult for you to let go of the past. But that's the good thing about me, Sarah. I'm a patient man. Whenever you decide to take me up on my offer . . . I'll be waiting.'

Her eyes searched his face, and there was a curious sense of wonder in them. 'I do believe you will be,' she replied. 'I really *do*.'

Impulsively she stepped into his arms then, and he planted a quick, chaste kiss on her cheek, knowing that whatever they had seen in and felt for each other, whatever feelings had developed between them in these past several hours, were too precious and too special to risk. Jack would take things one step at a time.

He climbed into the Toyota and studied mother and son from his window. Then he smiled and nodded, started the engine and said, 'Look after each other, you two.'

'We'll see you real soon, Jack!' called Ryan.

'You'd better, son.'

And as he drove away, Jack swallowed hard and felt his own spirits lift and continue lifting . . . because he knew that what Ryan had said was true. He *would* see them again, and it *would* be soon. And if the Fates were kind to him, it would also be forever.

Part Two

A Picture-Perfect Past

1

It's been exactly two hundred and thirteen days since Margot left me.

Two hundred and thirteen days of heartache and sorrow. Heartache and sorrow are effective fuel for power ballads and folksy love songs strummed on acoustic guitars, and also extremely influential in the formation of thought-provoking, heart-breaking lyrics; however, since I haven't played guitar in public since my freshman year of college, and since I spend eight hours a day in a gray three-sided cubicle, heartache and sorrow are useless to me.

'Jay. Jay. Jay!'

I turned my head to see Mr. Luu leaning against the entrance of my cube, wearing sharply pleated khakis, a white button-down shirt with short sleeves, and a red paisley tie. It's a look favoured by Mormons on mission and insurance salesmen; we are the latter, specifically car insurance. His left hand was positioned on his hip with his right hand resting on the top of the cube. His gold pinky ring dangled over the wall, his thumbnail fiddling with it. Mr. Luu is a short man. In order to maintain this pose he has to raise his arm higher than what would seem comfortable, and since I'm sitting at my desk, I'm forced to look up into his armpit. It's this type of posturing that helps him make up for his five-foot-five frame. He utilizes his strengths, which appear to be mostly non-verbal and include the element of surprise, hovering, and copious amounts of annoyed staring. He frightens me.

Margot used to say I was too timid and that I needed to stand up to him. 'You're six-five,' she'd say. 'Act like it.' What does she know?

'Yes, sir?' I finally respond.

'What are you doing?' Mr. Luu is Chinese, but he's been in the U.S. his entire life. He was raised in Brooklyn and has a heavy east coast accent. After attending a midwestern university and marrying a midwestern girl, he stayed in the midwest. It's impossible to hide your surprise when you hear him speak for the first time. I love to watch the slight widening in our clients' eyes when they meet him in person, after speaking with him on the phone. I'm sure his appearance has no resemblance to what they pictured. The tiny part in their lips, a clear indication of the urge to smile, is impossible to disguise no matter how intensely their respectful nature restrains them. Mr. Luu either doesn't notice or, being so used to this response, ignores it.

The question he's posed, standing here in my cube with all the power afforded him by the insurance commission and the Great State Insurance Company, is obviously a trick one. The truth: I was rehashing the final conversation I had with Margot, which, as I mentioned, took place two hundred and thirteen days ago in the living room of our apartment. *Our* apartment. This is technically true, as her name is still on the lease, but since she's no longer living there, having abandoned me, I guess it's just my apartment.

Regardless, I still have to answer his question. 'Nothing,' I say. It was my only option. I didn't even have a file open on my desk to pretend to be busy with.

'That's right, Jay, nothing. Why, Jay, why? Why are you doing nothing when there is a whole stack of something to be doing?' He was still playing with his pinky ring.

'I'll get right to it, Mr. Luu.' I scanned the stack of files that sat on the edge of my desk. I was shocked at the height to which it had risen. 'Um, which file are you most eager for?' It was an honest question but one that stopped Mr. Luu in mid-pinky ring twirl. He looked at me, then at the stack, rolled his eyes and walked away. I shrugged it off and went back to mentally rehashing my conversation with Margot until I could no longer avoid the pile of work on my desk. The sight of it was beginning to give me an anxiety attack. At that point I decided my only option was to leave my cube. *Coffee and a smoke*, I thought. Coffee and smoking are the two valid reasons for someone to be away from their desk. No one seems to question the need for caffeine or nicotine; it's just understood.

The remainder of the morning rolled on in a similar way, until the clock finally indicated it was lunchtime. And lunch was usually spent in much of the same way as my breaks — cigarettes, coffee, and sulking. Sometimes I'd throw in a turkey sandwich. After all that I'd return to my cube and spend the afternoon the way I'd spent the morning — rehashing the Margot conversation, avoiding stack of work, ingesting caffeine, and inhaling nicotine. I'd grown comfortable in my routine.

But today was different. When I

entered my cube I saw a bright green file folder sitting on my desk. There was a sticky note attached with the words: *Open, Go,* written in Sharpie. I'm a simple guy. I don't get excited about much, but against the traditional beige manila folders that litter our office, the vibrant green of this one might as well have been a flashing neon sign. It piqued my curiosity. There was no question as to whether or not I'd open it; the sticky note was just superfluous, the green promised something unusual and I needed a bit of unusual in my life. As for the *go* portion of the note, that would remain to be seen. I've never been much of a *go* person.

I scanned the contents. It was a straightforward claim. A client had been in a fender bender and ended up with a broken trunk. I don't go out on claims calls very often. I'm only sent out when the claim happens to be in cities not specifically assigned to any particular agent. These are usually hard-to-find-on-a-map-type of towns, tiny little specks I end up spending hours looking for while the GPS just spins and spins looking for service.

I picked up the file and walked it down to Mr. Luu's office. He was on the phone but his door was open. My gentle rap on the window got his attention, but he didn't seem happy to see me. For a moment we just stared at each other. I held up the green folder and shrugged. Shrugging, the universal sign for: *What gives?* He shrugged back and I took his return gesture to say: *What gives with you?* Then he waved me off with his hands. I turned, packed up my things and left the office.

2

Milford isn't as obscure as some of the other towns I've been sent to. It's supposedly a quaint little town with lots of antique shops and little cafés. Margot had suggested taking a drive out there once. We'd actually gotten into an argument about it.

It was a sunny Saturday morning. We were sitting on the balcony of our . . . my . . . the apartment, drinking coffee and reading the paper. I couldn't imagine wanting to go or do anything other than what we were doing right then. To me, moments like that are to be savoured. They're pure perfection.

'Look, Jay.' Margot held up an ad publicizing a little festival in the town of Milford. 'Wanna go?'

I looked over at the ad. 'Really? Why?' I couldn't relate to her desire to interrupt this moment.

She took a deep breath and rolled her eyes. 'No reason, never mind.' She was mad and immediately I felt a wall go up between us.

'You don't have to get pissy about it. If you really want to go fine, let's go. I just thought we were having a nice time doing this.' I gestured to the table and the coffee and the paper scattered about. I lit a cigarette and settled back in my chair. This wasn't the first time we'd argued about this. Our ideas of leisure time were, and presumably still are, wildly different.

She looked at me with a face I'd never seen before, but one I started seeing almost every day until the final day, two hundred and thirteen days ago. It wasn't an angry face or even one that conveyed annoyance. It was defeat. 'You're right. Doing nothing is fine. Just fine.'

She stood up and slipped a smoke from the pack. She climbed onto the brick of the balcony ledge and leaned against the wall that divided us from our neighbours. I hated it when she did that. I had horrible visions of her falling to her death. I usually made her get down, but that day I knew I'd better keep my mouth shut.

★ ★ ★

I followed the roundabout onto Main Street. The fountain at its centre shot water up into the sky. I wondered how many accidents had been caused by distracted drivers focused on the display of water as opposed to the road. *Dangerous*, I thought, *very dangerous*.

My car crawled slowly down the street. It was the type of street that demanded a leisurely pace. I passed a café with a bright yellow awning. A couple sat beneath it at a white wicker table, enjoying what I presumed to be cappuccinos, or mochas, or some other over-priced fancy coffee drink served in oversized mugs. They looked happy and a wave of bitterness swelled inside me — *show offs*.

The quaintness of the town was almost too sweet to be real. There were several antique shops, kitschy boutiques, a florist, and a pastry shop with a four-tiered cake in the window. Several people were out strolling down the sidewalk with packages, their kids and dogs in tow. There was a family walking with ice cream cones. The father was laughing loudly at his son, whose ice cream was dripping down his shirt. *You've got to be kidding me*, I thought. I didn't believe this sort of charm actually existed. It seemed like a movie set. A shot of regret filled me. Margot would have loved this.

I found Mrs. Catt's and pulled into a spot right in front of the store. There were three parking spots designated for her shop's use. At the end of each stall stood a different tree — a cactus, a palm, and a small lemon, each with a sign dangling around its trunk that said: Mrs. Catt's Curiosities. I pulled into the cactus stall. I took a few minutes to gather my things, although there wasn't much to gather — just the file and my phone — but I spent another few seconds debating whether or not I should grab another smoke before I entered. As I sorted through this decision, leaning heavily toward another smoke, a tap on the window startled me so badly I threw the file folder against the windshield and yelled. 'Ahhh!'

I looked over to see an old lady standing outside my window. My outburst didn't seem to faze her. She just stood there smiling at me.

I offered an uneasy smile in return and rushed to pick up the scattered papers.

She rapped on the window again. I held up a finger to let her know I'd be with her momentarily. However, it appeared as though my non-verbal communication hadn't been clear enough. She rapped on the window again, only this time with a little more force.

'Yes, I'll be with you in a moment.'

'I can't hear you,' she said. 'You have

to get out of the car or I won't be able to help you, son.'

She was a little woman with silver hair piled high up on her head. A pair of glasses hung from her neck on a jewelled chain. She wore a simple blue dress covered by an elaborately decorated yellow apron trimmed in white. Giant red pockets in the shape of hearts were sewn onto the front. The pockets were stretched to their limits, obviously stuffed with something, although with what was anyone's guess.

I eased myself out of the car. Since she didn't step back, or even sideways, I had to squeeze myself between her and my car door. I towered over her. She looked up at me, then back down at my feet, then around me to my car, which, I've failed to mention, is about the size of a child's toy: two-door, Japanese, economy.

'It's a bit like clowns in the circus, isn't it, son?'

'A bit, yes.'

'Well, never mind; I'm just glad you

finally got out.' She slipped her arm through mine and began patting my forearm. She looked me up and down. 'Oh my, sweetheart, you are quite lovely, aren't you.'

'Thank you.' She was a cute old lady.

'No need to thank me, I just tell it like it is.' We were still walking arm and arm. 'I'm so glad you decided to come. I was worried you'd never get out of that car, which was quite worrisome. I wouldn't have been able to help you, you see.'

'Oh, well, actually, Mrs. Catt, I'm here to help you.'

She cut me off with a little giggle. 'Nonsense. Come along.'

I wasn't quite sure what she meant by *nonsense*. 'You are Mrs. Catt, right?'

She stopped. I stopped. She slowly turned around and pulled her glasses up onto her nose and peered at me through the lenses. She looked at me with the same up-and-down method she'd used when I first got out of the car, starting at my toes, all the way up to my head, and back down again. 'Now, now, sweetheart, let's not be silly. I'm far too old for games.' She spun around with more energy than seemed possible for a woman of her age, though I couldn't say for sure just how old she was.

I did as I was told and followed her into the shop. I'd expected large wooden bureaus, mismatched china sets, and dusty old paintings, and I wasn't disappointed. There were pieces scattered all over the place; however, there were also random pieces that didn't seem to belong at all. For instance, there was a stuffed moose head hanging on the wall above a relatively new microwave and a tread-mill. There was a flat-screen computer monitor sitting on top of a stack of paving bricks next to a vintage wedding dress. Every item had a price tag and the prices seemed as irrelevant as the items in the store. The bricks were priced at ten dollars each, while the treadmill was priced at two dollars and had a note attached to it that read: *Works great*.

As I looked around and tried to make sense of what I was seeing, I felt something brush my leg. I jerked spastically and let out an embarrassing gasp. I looked down to see a large black cat licking her paw. The cat was obviously not concerned by my irrational response. 'Sorry,' I said, not sure if I was apologizing to the cat or its owner. Mrs. Catt assumed I was apologizing to the cat.

'She doesn't speak English you know. She's a cat, son.'

I coloured in embarrassment for my overreaction and for the subsequent apology.

'Isn't that right, Pet, my sweet kitty? You don't speak English.' She was stroking the cat's belly. She stood up and again addressed me. 'I haven't quite cracked the kitty code but I'm sure it will come to me eventually.' She wasn't smiling and I wasn't sure if I should. 'Now, son, where . . . is it?'

I didn't mind her calling me 'son'; I just thought it would be more professional to offer up my name. 'Jay. My name, it's Jay Randall.'

She looked as though she needed time to make sense of what I'd said; as though it was the most ridiculous thing she'd ever heard. 'You are a strange one, aren't you? Far worse off than I thought.'

Funny, I was thinking the same about you. I kept my thought to myself. 'Okay then, should we get started?' I held up the folder. 'I'm from Great State Insurance. You called about a claim.' I was following her around the store, watching her pick up items and put them down and shake her head in frustration. 'Mrs. Catt, is there someone else who handles your affairs, maybe someone else I could speak to?'

She laughed in a high-pitched, lilting voice and continued on with her hunt. 'Oh, son, I haven't had an affair in years. Oh, la di da, I've found it. Look, Pet, I've found it.' A large golden retriever came bounding over.

I wasn't sure what to address first — the fact that she'd misunderstood what I meant by affairs, the old camera she was trying to hand to me, or that she'd just referred to her dog by the same name as her cat. 'You call your dog and cat by the same name?'

She cocked her head and looked down at the dog sitting patiently by her feet. 'Well, it's all the same, isn't it?'

'Well no, not really.' I crouched down and invited Pet to come over for some attention. I'd always wanted a dog, but Margot was allergic. Pet licked my face then rolled to have his belly scratched. I looked up to see Mrs. Catt smiling down at me. She bent down and scratched the dog's head.

'I can see I wasn't wrong about you. You'll be just fine. Here you go — take it, it's yours.' She forced the camera into my hand.

'Mrs. Catt, this is not why I'm here. I think you may have me confused with someone else.'

She patted her bun and smoothed her apron. She reached into her pocket and came out with a small dog bone. She bent down to give it to the dog but before she could she realized the dog was gone and the cat was back. 'Oh for goodness sake.' She reached back into her pocket and came out with a cat treat.

I stood there in stunned silence. I stared at the cat. 'Where did the dog go?'

Again she ignored me. 'Now, son, take the camera and go. It's time.'

'But, but —'

'Now really, Jay Randall, I can't spend all day with you. There are others.'

'But —'

She slipped her arm through mine and began walking me to the door. 'Off you go. Let's get moving. I know movement is difficult for you, but for goodness sake, Jay Randall, this is getting ridiculous.'

I wasn't sure what was happening. I

looked around for a television crew; maybe I was on some sort of show.

'Oh wait!' she said. 'I almost forgot. It's two dollars.'

'What?'

'The camera, it's two dollars. You didn't think it was free, did you? Adjustment will have to cost you something or you won't take it seriously. Think of it as an investment.'

Her philosophy reminded me of the man at the gym who said the high cost of gym membership was partly because if people paid for the service they'd feel compelled to use it. I slipped my hand into my pocket and handed her two crumpled dollar bills. It was worth it to get out of the store and back to the safety of my tiny car.

She shoved the dollars into her apron pocket. I had a brief vision of my dollar bills mingling with the dog-cat treats.

We walked side by side. She'd slipped her arm through mine again, as though she instinctively knew I'd need the guidance.

I was in a daze. She walked me all the way to the car, patting my arm. 'Alrighty, then, here we are, back at the beginning.' I looked at her, trying to make sense of what had just happened. She wasn't returning my gaze. She was waving to someone else on the other side of the street. I turned to see an average-looking man sweeping up in front of his store. He had stopped sweeping and was waving back to Mrs. Catt with a broad grin. His lack of alarm was comforting. 'That's Mr. Jones. He's such a flirt.'

I couldn't help but laugh at her feistiness. I'd always been a sucker for the senior community. They can get away with whatever they want. I fumbled with my keys. When I finally got the door open I folded myself back into my car. As I did so, I realized Mrs. Catt was already on the doorstep of her shop.

'Is that a parrot?' I spoke out loud to my empty car as I stared at her through the windshield.

'You're in the car now, son. I can't hear you,' she yelled. The parrot on her shoulder flared its wings in response to her shouting. I rolled down my window to let some fresh air in and watched her stroke the parrot's back. 'Settle down, Pet, settle down.'

I started the car and backed out as quickly as possible with one hand on the steering wheel and the other fumbling for a cigarette.

3

The drive home consisted of chain smoking, trying to figure out what had just happened, and an occasional glance at the old camera on my passenger seat. The Nikon logo seemed to be begging someone to wipe the dirt from its proud letters.

I didn't bother going back to the office. I wasn't sure I could handle it. This realization bugged me; I hated how fragile I'd become.

I got home before I knew it and without really remembering the drive. I walked through the door, and for the first time in two hundred and thirteen days, I wasn't startled by the starkness of my apartment. When it was *our* apartment, it was filled with colour. The small space had always reminded me of a jar of jellybeans — paintings, photographs, small decorative pillows, pops of colour all over the place. When Margot left, the colour left with her. She left me with beige.

I sat at the round pinewood table in the space the apartment manager had called the dining room. I reached for a cigarette and was stunned that the pack was empty. Frustrated, I started fumbling with the camera. It was old. I assumed it was from the fifties or sixties. I'd have to research it to know for sure. The plastic had gotten grimy from years of dust and deterioration. It felt greasy. Instinctively, I held it up to my eye. The viewfinder was fuzzy and too dirty to see through, but the lens turned easily and smoothly; as I rotated it a blurry image of the balcony moved back and forth toward my eye.

This camera had been someone's exciting new purchase, I thought. I wondered what the person had felt when they'd taken it out of the store; I wondered what photos had been produced, and finally I wondered about the person who'd arranged the purchase with Mrs. Catt, only to arrive there and realize she'd given it to someone else. *Strange woman*, I thought. I fiddled with the rewind crank and felt resistance. There was film in it. I continued to crank until it clicked. The back popped open to reveal an old canister of film. I rolled the ancient spool of Kodak between my fingertips and understood I held someone's memories in my hand. I closed my hand around it and reached for a cigarette.

'Ugh,' I grumbled in frustration. I'd already forgotten I was out.

★   ★   ★

I walked into the drug store with a bitter need for cigarettes, the film in my pocket. The store smelled like candy. I marvelled at the countless bags of sweets that lined the shelves. I'd always loved drug stores. It's a guilty pleasures haven. I walked past the aisles of creamy cosmetics, past the greeting cards, beyond the rows and rows of booze and finally arrived to the back of the store where the neon sign hanging on the back wall advertised one-hour photo.

The photo centre was being manned by a teenage boy sporting a bull-ring in his nose. He was sitting on the back counter next to the photo-processing machine with his nose buried in an *Auto Trader*. He hadn't seen me come up. I stood there for a few seconds hoping he'd realize I was in his presence. He didn't.

'I'd like to have this developed,' I said, holding up the canister.

He looked up as if he'd been caught off guard. 'Oh, dude, sorry, I didn't see you there.' He was surprisingly pleasant. I was expecting attitude. He hopped off his perch and walked over to the counter. He reminded me of myself, without the piercing and long hair. He was tall and lanky. Dark brown hair hung around his shoulders. He could have passed for my little brother.

He pointed to the end of the counter. 'Just fill out one of those . . . wait, dude, let me see that.' He'd caught sight of the canister and took it from my hand. 'Dude, are you sure?'

'Um, yeah, I guess. What do you mean am I sure?'

'Okay, dude, I can't promise it will work, but I'll give it a go.'

'What, is it too old or something?'

'Uh, yeah,' the kid said, as though he was really not sure how to respond. 'Something like that. *It is really old.*'

'Well, just do what you can.'

'No problem.' The kid was grinning. It wasn't an unpleasant sarcastic kind of grin, like you expect to see on punk kids. It was an expectant grin, a knowing grin. It was unsettling.

'It won't take long,' he said through his smile. 'You're the only job I have.'

'Okay, well, I'm going to go do a little shopping and I'll be back in . . . ' I let my voice trail off, expecting him to fill in the space.

He took the cue. 'Oh, uh, like twenty minutes I guess.'

'Okay, good.'

I bolted straight toward the cigarettes, bought a carton, and headed for the door. I smoked one greedily as soon as I reached the pavement. The day before she left me, Margot told me she was quitting. I told her I'd quit too. I'd been meaning to since, well, for too long. I replayed the exchange in my mind. The look she gave me when I told her I'd quit expressed her doubt.

Now, I looked down at the cigarette in my hand and figured she'd known she was leaving, and she knew I'd never make it through the breakup without nicotine.

I went back into the store after smoking one more. The kid at the photo centre saw me coming and looked pleased with himself.

'I think you'll like these,' he said. 'I didn't get them all, but I got a few really good ones, nice and clear. Did you know her? Is she like your mom or something?'

I looked at him, confused. It took me a moment to realize what he was getting at. 'Oh, uh, no, I don't know who the film belongs to. I just sort of stumbled upon it.'

'Ah,' the kid said, shaking his head perceptively, 'curiosity got the better of you.' He was smiling as though he sees that sort of thing all the time.

I instantly thought of Mrs. Catt's and her curiosity shop. 'Yes, I suppose so.'

'Cool. Well, good luck.'

'Yeah, thanks.'

4

I left the photos in the paper sleeve until I got home. Habit usually dictated that I smoke as soon as I walked in the front door, but I couldn't wait to see what waited for me in the packet of photos. The urge for a cigarette never struck.

I pulled out the small stack of photos. Most of them were covered in large blotches with orange edges. It looked as though the photos were melting and someone froze them midway through the process.

I flipped through the first few quickly and finally arrived at the five photos that had survived. That's when I saw her. The photos were in colour, but the images were faded and soft. Not like the bright pops of colour we get in photos today. The woman was young, twenties maybe. I guessed she was close to my age, twenty-five, or something like that. Her auburn hair was pulled back from her face by a thick black headband and it flipped up at the ends, finishing with a bounce at her shoulders. She was wearing a yellow dress that was cinched at the waist by a band of the same yellow fabric. It had a small yellow bow at the centre. She had a beautiful smile that she flashed playfully for the camera. She was outside in a field; a blanket was spread out on the ground, and some black pumps had been tossed aside. The photographer had captured the joy and light-heartedness of the moment. I guessed the photographer was a man, that he was in love with her and that she returned the favor. One image caught her blowing a kiss to the lens, one showed her holding her hands in the shape of a heart, another was of her reaching out toward the camera, and my favourite was of her sitting on the blanket, her dress billowing around her. She wasn't posing; he'd caught her in mid-thought.

I think it's funny how people try to guess what was in the minds of people in photographs or paintings, as if any of us really knows what the subject of the Mona Lisa was actually thinking, but as I looked at the image of this beautiful woman I couldn't help but wonder. She was looking down at the blanket as if she were trying to figure out how it had been woven, or maybe she'd spotted an ant and was watching it make its way across the fibers to their picnic. I wanted to know. I found myself being bothered by not knowing what her thoughts were. Her head was turned in a way that revealed just her profile and it was the only photo in which she wasn't smiling.

The last picture was of her and the photographer together. I was right, it was a man, but he'd only managed to get the bottom half of his face in the frame. It was clear though, from the way they were huddled up next to each other, his free arm wrapped around her waist, his leg intertwined with hers, that they were definitely in love. It was irrational, but for some reason I felt a twinge of jealousy as I stared at their image. I didn't want her to love him, and I certainly didn't want them to be touching. It was a possessive pose; she was holding on to his arm tightly as though she were afraid he'd float away. He was wearing a white t-shirt and jeans. I was amused at how, amidst all the changes since the middle of the century, the uniform of the casual man remains the same: White tee and Levi's.

The boyfriend — that's what I'd started calling him in my mind, as opposed to the photographer — had a rebellious half-smile on his face. His smile looked like it belonged to a man who knew he was going to get lucky and was gloating about it. It was a familiar smile, but I couldn't place it. All I knew was, I was beginning to dislike him very much. His other arm, the one that wasn't gripping her, was outstretched. His hand disappeared from the frame; obviously it held the camera that now sat on my table. I put that picture back to the end of the stack and returned my focus to the image of her on the blanket.

I stared at her profile longer than would seem necessary for a normal person. When I finally peeled my eyes away, I stuck the image to the fridge, made myself some dinner, and went to bed.

5

It took too long to fall asleep. My thoughts were anchored in a field with a beautiful woman and a romantic picnic. I ached for Margot. Why couldn't Margot and I have created that kind of love? I thought about the boyfriend — the way he seemed to possess her, the way he knew exactly when to snap the photo. He celebrated her. Did Margot want me to possess her? Did she feel celebrated by me? I drifted to sleep with regret on my mind.

When I woke I thought I heard the rustlings of Margot in the kitchen. I often woke up forgetting that she was gone, but today I had actually convinced myself that I heard her. My eyes shot open as I remembered she was gone and that I was alone. I fumbled out of bed, tripping on the sheets that I'd kicked off in the night. I splashed water on my face, brushed my teeth and made my way to the kitchen for coffee. I was silently thanking God it was Saturday.

I got as far as the entry to the kitchen and froze. There was a woman standing in front of the refrigerator staring at the photo.

'Excuse me?' I spoke softly. I didn't want to startle her. Maybe she'd stumbled in after a hard night of partying and got confused as to which apartment was hers. She turned around and surprise registered on her face. My body seized in shock, and every muscle tensed.

'Holy . . . ' My hand flew to my mouth. 'What the . . . Holy . . . I mean you're her. How are you . . . ' I walked over to the photo and pointed at it. 'You're her,' I repeated.

'Yes, I know.' Her voice was sweet and soft.

'But how? Why?' I was beginning to feel dizzy. My hands drifted to the top of my head. I was beginning to hyperventilate. I blinked rapidly, trying to adjust my vision. She remained calm. She brought Margot's favourite pink porcelain mug to her lips. The letter M, written in black cursive, was facing me. Somehow, in the midst of the chaos occurring in my mind, I was able to notice how odd the mug looked in someone else's hands. 'I'm having a nervous breakdown, right? You're like, not really here. Right?'

I was really starting to lose consciousness now, so I sat down at the table and threw my head between my knees. It's what I'd heard you're supposed to do.

'A nervous breakdown,' she said, 'would that really be better?' She had bent herself at the waist, hanging her head upside down so she could look me in the face. The tips of her hair brushed the linoleum.

I lifted my head up and looked at her. She tilted her head to the side and smiled the same beautiful smile from the photos.

'No, I suppose a nervous breakdown wouldn't be better.'

She walked over to the counter and set Margot's mug down. 'I helped myself to some coffee. I hope you don't mind. There was a full pot, which I was grateful for because I don't think I'd have been able to figure out that contraption. It's like the Jetsons or something.'

'It has a timer. It brews a full pot every morning before I even get up. I don't like to wait for my first cup of coffee.' *Why are we talking about coffee?* I thought.

She turned around and looked at the photo again. 'There are more,' I said.

'I know, I saw.' She turned around and gestured toward the living room where the coffee table held the camera and photos. When her arm swung out it startled me. I instinctively leaned away from her.

'Do I frighten you?

'Yes, of course.'

'I'm not a ghost, you know.'

'What are you?'

She considered this for a moment. 'I'm just me.'

She didn't seem as alarmed by her presence as I was. She seemed comfortable, as if this had been a planned visit. I stood up to get my own cup of coffee. I needed to get a hold of myself. My movement caught her attention. 'You're really tall.'

In spite of my confusion and dismay, I laughed. 'Yeah, I know.' I reached for a mug and tried to pour the coffee, but my nerves were causing me to shake so badly that the carafe rattled against the mug. She came over and took it out of my hand and poured me a cup.

'You're not exactly the man of steel, are you? You really need to get a hold of yourself. You're a wreck.'

'I don't think that's a very fair assessment. I don't have much experience with waking up to find a woman who popped out of an old photograph in my kitchen.' My voice had an edge to it that I hadn't really intended, but I was stressed and frustrated, and a little put off. She was criticizing my ability to cope with . . . with . . . what exactly? What was happening?

'Do you think *I* have experience with this sort of thing?' she asked.

'I have no idea.' At this point our voices were at the precipice of yelling. The tone didn't necessarily sound angry, but our voices did have an air of major anxiety to them. Basically, we were freaking out. 'Why are we yelling?' I shouted.

'I don't know!' She shouted back.

We just looked at each other for a moment. Our breath was ragged, and our faces were set with an intense glare. I took a second to see her, to look at her in full view. She was dressed differently than she was in the photo. She wore a sleeveless linen dress that fell just above her knees. Her hair wasn't curled at the ends anymore. She looked like she could be any one of Margot's friends.

She interrupted my assessment. 'Do

you know why I'm here?' Her voice was soft now.

I wasn't sure if she knew the answer and was testing me to see if I knew as well, or if she was hoping I could enlighten her. She refilled her coffee and walked into the living room. She picked up the photos I'd left on the table.

'You seem really . . .'

'Really what?' She looked up from the photos.

'Really at ease. I mean, for someone who isn't supposed to be here . . . in this place . . . this decade.' It was true. She had a sense of lightness about her that I'd never known for myself. I seem to have a cloud of melancholy surrounding me at most times, not depression or gloominess necessarily, just a certain amount of dreariness.

'She sort of prepared me,' she said. She didn't look up from the pictures. Her pictures. She was sitting on the couch, and it occurred to me that the couch was probably the only thing in the apartment that felt familiar to her — that and the pictures. The couch was the first thing Margot and I had purchased together. It was a pale yellow couch with dark wood legs that were shaped like cones. It was built in 1960 and we'd purchased it from a vintage furniture dealer. Margot fell in love with it. She used to say she was born in the wrong decade. She believed she was a misplaced mid-century citizen. I couldn't understand her fascination with the past until I found these photos. There seemed to be a joy back then that just isn't in existence anymore.

'Who? Who sort of prepared you?' I asked her.

'Mrs. Catt.' She looked up at me as if I should've known the answer. 'She's a real trip, isn't she?'

6

I wasn't completely surprised. Since entering the crazy woman's shop, irrationality had ensued.

'You've been to see Mrs. Catt?' I asked.

'I brought her the camera.'

'When? Why?'

'Well, as for when, it was yesterday, only I guess it wasn't yesterday. It was yesterday fifty years ago.'

She was still flipping through the pictures while she spoke. I couldn't tell if her expression reflected fondness or sorrow.

'How can that be? What year exactly?'

'Nineteen sixty-two, and I have no idea how it can be. All I know is I went to sell her this camera. She took it from me and gave me this key.' She reached into her dress pocket and took out a key. It had a slip of paper attached to it by a piece of yarn. The paper had my address written on it.

She stopped there. I waited for her to continue but she didn't. She just stared at the photos. I envied her stillness. I would not be as serene if I woke up in a different decade. 'How are you so calm?'

She looked up at me. 'You're calm.'

Touché, I thought. She was right, at the moment I did *appear* calm. Although, as she said it, I realized I had my hand on top of my head, which Margot always said was my stress stance. It usually involved a cigarette too.

'I'm freaking out on the inside.'

'Me too,' she said with a smile that was comforting enough to bring my hand away from my head. I sat down next to her. We looked at the photos together. She now had them spread out on the table in front of us. We looked in silence until I reached out and touched the one of her blowing a kiss.

'You look so happy. What's it like to

be that happy, to have that kind of love?' The question hung in the air for a moment.

She reached for the photo and our fingers brushed. She didn't seem to mind, so I didn't pull my hand away. I wanted to feel her skin to be sure she was real. She was real. She was definitely real.

'I wouldn't know.'

I didn't acknowledge her response; I didn't want to press her. She took my hand in hers and shook it. 'Cece,' she said, 'Chambers.'

'Jay Randall.'

'Jay,' she said, 'it looks like we've got some work to do.'

'Yes, I guess we do.'

She leaned back and rested her head against the back of the couch. She brought her coffee to her perfect lips. Is it possible to be envious of a coffee mug? She closed her eyes. 'Nice couch,' she said.

I leaned back and rested my head. 'Thanks.'

7

We walked into Mrs. Catt's. Pet, the dog, came bounding up. Cece bent down and took his head in her hands. She rubbed his head and drool spilled out of his mouth onto her arm. She didn't seem to care. It didn't bother her. I decided this made her likeable.

'Hello little Pet, where's your mommy?' Cece spoke to Pet in the tone of voice that people use when speaking to animals.

'Well, isn't this a surprise.' From the back of the store Mrs. Catt came striding. She walked around a huge mahogany elephant, and dodged a small red tricycle. 'Of course, not completely a surprise, since everyone always returns, but I thought you two might be the exception. Well never mind, the policy is the policy and I can't make any exceptions — no exchanges, no returns.'

Cece and I looked at one another. I could see my feelings written on her face — confusion.

I decided I'd be the one to get to the bottom of this. I was going to sort it out in a professional manner.

'Mrs. Catt, we just . . . well, you see . . . um, we're totally confused and we're hoping you'll be . . . ' I was stumbling and desperately hoping Mrs. Catt would come to my rescue and simply explain what magic spell she'd placed on us, but she didn't let me off the hook. She let me struggle. She looked me right in the eye and just blinked at me while I tried to sort out the words I needed to explain what it was that Cece and I were hoping to accomplish.

'Yes, what is it? Continue on, son.' She seemed exasperated.

Cece took a crack at it. 'Well, you see Mrs. Catt, I brought you the camera the other day.'

'Yes.'

'Well, then you sold it to Jay.'

'Yes, dear, that's the way this works. Really children, I haven't any time for this. What is it you want?'

'Well, how did you do it?' Cece and I spoke in unison.

She looked at us as if she didn't understand the question.

'Is it some sort of spell? Is there a way to break it?' I asked.

She giggled. 'Oh dear, a spell? Do you take me for a witch? Oh my.' She continued to giggle. 'I sell things to people who need them, that's all. Someone brings something in, I buy it and sell it to someone else.'

'No, Mrs. Catt, we understand that, it's just . . . ' At that point I interrupted myself as Cece gasped. Pet, who a moment ago was a slobbering yellow dog, now appeared to be a yellow canary. He flew up onto the trunk of the mahogany elephant, and it's little black eyeballs blinked innocently at us. Cece and I stared.

'Go on, son, what is it you want to know?'

'Uh, um . . .'

'Oh for heaven's sake. If you run into the wind you'll just exhaust yourself. Now then, just turn around, and let the wind push you along.' She put her hands on the small of our backs and gently turned us toward the door. 'What's done is done, all sales are final, no returns, no exchanges.'

Stunned, we made our way back to my car, which was now a resting spot for Pet — the black cat.

'Here, Pet, get off the car. Sorry about that, he just does whatever he pleases.'

'That's what she's sorry about,' I mumbled under my breath. 'That's what she addresses.'

'Well, that went well,' Cece said, as we backed out of the stall, 'don'tcha think?'

'Hmph.'

'I tried to tell you that we wouldn't get anywhere with her.' There was an amused tone to her voice. Without even looking at her, I could tell she was smiling. She had, in fact, tried to convince me that going to Mrs. Catt would be futile. 'She isn't going to help us; you must know this,' she'd said. But I couldn't just sit and do nothing. Action, we had to take action.

I felt irritation rising up through my body. Then I looked over at her. She had her bare feet up on my dashboard. Why this was so intoxicating is unclear, but the mere sight of her toes made me relax. I continued to make my case, trying to make Cece understand our dilemma. She was obviously in shock. 'This is a really big deal, you know, mainly for you. I mean, for me, it just means I've lost my mind. But you, you've lost your life; the world you knew is gone. Gone, Cece. Gone, never . . . '

'Yeah, I got it, Jay.' She sat up and dropped her feet.

I wanted her feet to come back. 'Sorry, I just don't understand you, or this; I just need things to make sense.'

'What in life ever makes sense, Jay? I haven't had a life that makes sense since I was eleven. My life has been a mess. I . . . oh forget it.'

She had a story she wasn't ready to tell and I wasn't about to push her. 'Sorry,' I said again, feeling completely inept. 'You can put your feet back on the dash.'

She glared at me suspiciously from the corner of her eye. 'You're not some creepy foot guy, are you?'

'No! Geez, no!' I was horrified. 'You were just happier —' *And so was I*, I thought, but didn't say. ' — when you had your feet on the dash and your arm out the window.'

She threw her head back, laughed, and put her feet back up on the dash. 'Oh, Jay, what are we going to do?'

8

We'd gotten back to the apartment and found ourselves right back to where we'd started before we'd left for Mrs. Catt's, heads resting on the back of the couch, and pictures spread out in front of us on the coffee table. We stayed like that for a long time, long enough for me to doze off and get a kink in my neck. It was only noon but it had been an exhausting morning.

I opened my eyes and stretched my neck. Cece stirred and sat up as if she'd been startled. Out of reflex I put my hand on her leg. 'Are you okay?'

She looked down at my hand and I instantly pulled it away. 'Yes, I just forgot where I was for a minute.'

'I can only imagine.'

She flashed her sweet smile. 'I'm starved,' she said.

'Me too.'

I suggested Watson's for lunch. I thought it would be the perfect place for a girl from the past. It's been in town since the fifties, and from what the pictures on the wall disclosed, hadn't changed much since then. She said Watson's was fine. 'We hang out there all the time,' she'd said.

We travelled the half-mile from the apartment to the diner on foot and in silence. Her head was everywhere but forward. She never stopped turning to see cars, the people, the storefronts; there was so much to take in. At one point I had to redirect her to save a caterpillar working its way across the sidewalk. She looked down to see why I'd stopped her then patted my chest. 'Ah, you're sweet.'

It was the smallest of affirmations and I realized how stupid it was to feel pride over it, but I did.

We slid into the booth and both ordered the lunch special: turkey on white, fries, and a coke. Her eyes scanned the restaurant and out the window and mine scanned her. She explored her new world and I was exploring mine. I didn't want to be caught staring, but I was entranced by the impossibility of her — the impossibility of her on several levels. One: her physical presence in this space of time. Two: her presence in my life. Girls like her do not turn up in my life unexpectedly. I have to work for them. Margot took some convincing. It's not that I'm unattractive, or socially awkward; I'm just plain. I'm turkey on white, fries and a coke. Margot was roasted red pepper, shaved prosciutto, and soft mozzarella, topped with arugula and a pesto aioli. She never believed she was my type. She used to say that I only liked the idea of her. At the time I hadn't understood what that meant. She was always trying out new philosophical ideas. But now, sitting across from Cece, I began to understand what Margo had meant. I had really liked the idea of Cece when she was an image on a photo, but did I really want her, the person, the live physical being? Well, she did order turkey on white, so maybe there was potential. What was I thinking? The poor girl was stuck in a foreign land without any hope of return and I sat wondering if she was my type and if she'd go for me. What a jerk.

'Okay,' she said abruptly, 'let's start from the beginning.' She pushed her plate aside, folded her hands on the table and looked me in the eye. 'Why do you have my pictures?'

'That's the beginning?' I asked.

'Maybe.'

There was a piece of hair falling over her eye. I wanted to reach across the table and tuck it behind her ear like a scene from a romantic comedy. She must have seen that my eyes had settled there because she reached up and did the job herself. Not that I would have; that's not my style, although I sometimes wished it were.

'Well?' she asked again. I was suddenly feeling embarrassed. Her question made me feel like a voyeur. In spite of my innocence, I felt a few beads of sweat forming on my forehead and I was suddenly aware of the sun streaming in on my face. She moved toward me to pull the shade down. She had to reach all the way across the table to my side of the booth. Her chest was inches from my face; I was riveted. *Oh my gosh, I am a voyeur.*

I quickly shifted my head and moved to the end of the booth. 'Thanks.'

'Sure.'

I couldn't look her in the eye.

'I make you uncomfortable.' It wasn't a question; it was a statement.

I forced myself to look at her. 'I don't think it's you, I think it's the situation.'

She looked at me intently, as though she really wanted to understand me. It gave me confidence. 'Look, Cece, I'm not some weirdo that goes around developing random women's pictures and pinning them to my refrigerator hoping they'll show up in my kitchen. I had no idea you'd come looking for them.' Never in my life had I had such a mixture of emotions: anxiety, curiosity, frustration, desire and confidence. After I finished my statement we just looked at each other for a moment, then we both started laughing.

'Okay, so maybe I am some weird guy that goes around developing strange women's photos, but I don't do it on a regular basis. As a matter of fact I've never done it before in my life.'

'Okay, so maybe that's part of it.'

'What do you mean?'

'Listen, Jay, I don't know your whole story — I'm sure it's a doozy — but whatever it is we've been brought together for some specific reason, right? I mean I don't know about you, but I don't believe in random occurrences; it's too suspicious.'

She had a point, although I wasn't sure I liked her assuming my story was bad enough to be considered a doozy.

Did I give off some sort of I'm-way-messed-up-vibe or something?

She cocked her head to the side and narrowed her eyes. It took all my confidence not to look away. 'What possessed you to develop fifty-year-old film anyway?' she asked.

'I don't know really. I was just curious about who would get rid of a camera with undeveloped film still in it. It was kind of like a mystery I guess.' She kept listening, so I just kept on talking. It was getting awkward. 'And besides, Mrs. Catt was so intent on giving it to me I figured there must be a reason.' Nothing, no response. She just kept waiting for me to finish. 'It's not like I'm just nosy or anything. I actually do believe in people's privacy, you know.'

I had no idea what Cece was thinking. She was staring at me while I unravelled this tale, listening intently. And I mean actually hearing and processing what I was saying, as if she were really interested and not just waiting for her turn to talk. This made me nervous; the more I talked the more likely I was to stick my foot in my mouth. 'I guess I assumed the people who owned the thing were obviously uninterested.'

That last statement seemed to give her a reason to think. She looked up to the ceiling and then back at me as if she were trying to figure out whether or not what I'd said was true.

I decided it was my turn. 'Okay, so why did you get rid of the camera?'

She took a deep breath and let it out quickly with a slump of her shoulders like a frustrated child. 'He left it. I couldn't believe it when he did, but he did, he left it.' Then, almost as an afterthought and under her breath she said: 'I can't believe he wanted out that badly.' She looked at me again. 'But, he did. He wanted out that badly. He actually left everything behind, even the camera.' She was shaking her head in disbelief. 'He'd saved for that thing for a year. It was the best you could get at the time.'

Her face suddenly lost a bit of its light. Tears rested at the rim of her eyelids. I couldn't stand it. If she were mine I'd do everything in my power to never see that look again. As soon as she saw the pity in my face she straightened up.

'Yuck, I am so sorry. I'm not usually this sappy or silly.'

'Please don't apologize. I understand . . . too well unfortunately.'

Her eyes widened. 'That's it then, the thread that connects us.' Seeing my confusion, she continued. 'Heartbreak, Jay. We're connected by heartbreak.' She was smiling as she reached across the table and laid her hand on top of mine. 'Don't you see?'

What I saw — was her hand on mine. What I saw — was the smile on her face. What I saw — was impossible joy.

★   ★   ★

We walked through town slowly. We both claimed a desire to get to the

196

bottom of this situation, but other than a few details here and there, about the day we stepped through this crack in the universe, we kept the conversation to a minimum. It was as if we understood the fragility of the situation and neither of us wanted to break the spell. She didn't seem to be in a hurry to get back and I didn't want her to leave.

'Insurance, car insurance? That's what brought you to Mrs. Catt?'

'Yep. It's not very exciting, I know, but I found a file on my desk that directed me to her. It was clear though, once I got there, that she hadn't called for an insurance claim.'

'She's a gas, isn't she?'

I smiled at her antiquated slang. 'Yeah, a gas.'

'What is that?' She was pointing to someone's phone. 'Everyone has one.'

'They're phones.'

'What?'

'Yeah, they're phones and cameras,

and video recorders and calendars. They run the world.'

'That's the craziest.'

'Crazy — I used to think I understood what that meant, but now I have new respect for the word.'

We wandered into a park, and after a few moments she froze. 'Oh. My. Gosh. You've got be kidding?' She looked stunned.

'What?'

She was looking around the park. It was a beautiful space filled with perfectly manicured green grass, flowerbeds, fountains, benches and brass statues scattered throughout. The statues were life-size and depicted everyday citizens caught in the middle of various leisure activities. People frozen in time — children playing ball, a man fishing at the edge of the pond, a elderly woman on a park bench, all of them so lifelike they looked as though a simple touch would bring them to life. I held my breath as Cece walked over to a bench where a statue of an elderly woman sat. She studied it for a moment before reaching out to stroke the statue's cheek. I half expected her touch to bring the old lady to life, as though Cece was filled with whatever magic had brought her here.

'Fascinating,' she said.

We sat on the bench with the statue between us. The three of us — Cece, the statue, and me — sat quietly.

'This is Meadowlark Park, right? Corner of Spring St. and Fifth?

'Yeah, you remember it?'

'This is the park.'

'The park?' She was looking at me as though I should be able to figure out what she meant. I knew what she meant but it was hard to believe. 'From the photos? Really?' The park in the photos was sparse, and from what I could see, looked like it was covered in dry yellowing grass.

'Yep. We used to laugh because they'd named it Meadowlark Park and it was anything but meadowy or larky. It was just dry patches of grass and a few trees for shade. There wasn't even a playground. They always said . . . ' She paused and rolled her eyes. 'Whoever *they* are, that they were raising funds to make it a park worthy of its name. For years there was a sign that said something like: Future home of your favourite park. I guess they finally came through.'

'Yeah, I mean, I grew up here, and as far as I know it's always been meadowy and larky.'

She laughed at my use of her made-up words. 'You're funny.'

'I try.'

She looked around, scanning the park as though she were looking for Joey. 'It was our last good day, Joey and me. Joey and Cece. Cece and Joey. I think I always knew it wouldn't last. Nothing lasts for Joey.'

As she said it I wondered: *Did I always know it wouldn't last for Margot and me?*

'He was an artist. I loved that. He had a romantic and impractical view of life.' She thought for a moment. 'I didn't always love that part.' She paused then started laughing. It wasn't a maniacal, crazy person's laugh. It was a sweet giggle that makes it impossible for those around not to smile.

'What?' I asked.

'Oh, nothing. I was just thinking if Joey could see me now he'd never believe it. What an adventure I'm on.' Her smile turned downward. 'He'd probably just be irritated that it took so long.'

'What happened? You looked so happy in the pictures.'

'Picture-perfect right?' She gave a sarcastic laugh that didn't suit her. I wanted her sweet, joyful smile to come back.

'I take it that it wasn't so perfect.'

'At first it was amazing. Joey was all light and fire and energy. I loved how his hands were always splattered with paint or how he was always humming a tune or lost in thought, like he was creating something in his mind.'

We both looked out over park, and with the statue of the old lady between us, it felt almost like a confessional.

'Joey was fascinated by moments caught in time. He wanted to travel the world freezing moments, making music and creating art. I felt like just being in his presence was all the travel I needed.'

'Margot always talked about travelling the world.'

'Margot?'

'Yeah.'

'Oh, she must be the one who brought you to Mrs. Catt.'

'I guess so. Although I have no idea what that means.'

'I waited a year. I waited a whole year for him to come back. We'd gone to the park and he took my picture. He spent the day talking about all the places he wanted to see, paint, and photograph. He said he wanted me to be his muse in Paris, Cairo, Rome, and Madrid. The more he talked the more afraid I became. I think I always knew I'd never be enough for him. I was afraid I'd be abandoned in some foreign land.' She was silent for a moment and we both felt the irony of what she'd said. There couldn't be a more foreign land than this. 'I told him that night that I couldn't go. I was laying as close to him as possible, breathing in his air and curled around his lean body.'

I hated this description. I definitely did not want to picture her with this guy in bed. I could tell by the way she was talking that she was almost just thinking out loud, maybe just talking to the statue. She couldn't see my face, which I'm sure was plastered with an awkward grimace.

'I asked him to give me more time,' she said, 'to marry me first. But he hated any talk of marriage. He said it would strangle his creativity. I cried myself to sleep and he was gone in the morning. No note, no goodbye. All I had was this camera and a tree in this park where he'd carved our names. But even that wasn't perfect. He spelled my name with two capital Cs. I hate that. I looked at our names on the tree and how proud he was of the gesture, and all I could think was, he should know I hate that.' She looked out at the park and I could tell she was looking for the tree, but she gave up. There was no way it was still here. It was evident they'd cleared the space before rebuilding the park.

I thought about the last day with Margot and the tears we both cried, the fight that raged, and the desperation in my voice as I asked her to stay. 'I think it's easier that way. Joey's way, I mean. Like ripping off a bandage.'

'Maybe,' she said. 'But why leave me with the camera; why leave the last happy day behind for me to see forever? That's just mean.'

I thought about Joey and Margot and how similar their passions were. 'I wonder if Joey's with Margot some-where in an alternate universe. He sounds like her type.'

Cece laughed. 'You *really* are funny.' She jumped up and held her hands out to me. 'Stand up.'

I laid my hands on hers and mine covered hers entirely. I stood up and kept hold of one of her hands. It was an uncharacteristically bold move, but she didn't pull away. We walked hand in hand through the park.

'We're the boring ones,' I said. Cece laughed.

She really does think I'm funny, I thought.

9

We stood at the edge of the pond, her hand still in mine.

'Mrs. Catt — did you know her before you brought her the camera?' I asked.

'Not personally, just her reputation. Joey used to talk about her all the time — the trippy old lady from Milford.'

'She was old back then?' I asked.

'Yeah, silver hair, big apron, grandma-type, just like now. As a matter of fact she looks exactly the same.'

'She must be ancient now, but I can't really tell for sure. Every aspect of her is confusing.'

'She was waiting for me. When I walked in she said: Well, well, well, Miss Chambers, it took you long enough. Hand it over, but only if you're sure.'

'That's it?'

'No, then she said I needed to be

sure because I could never reverse it.'

'That's intense.'

'Yeah, but she also said she didn't think I'd want to. At first I thought she was talking about taking back the camera — you know, like she said: All sales are final. But then she took hold of my arm, and I swear I saw a light flash in her eye, like a little twinkle. Then she said something about it being a bumpy ride.' She thought for a moment. 'But then she also said that someone would be there to help me.' As she said this, she squeezed my hand. 'That would be you I guess.'

Her voice was soft and a little unsure as she said all this. Her fragility stirred an instinctual protectiveness in me that I'd never known before, and I liked it. I never felt like any of the girls I'd dated needed protection. Margot certainly never did. The thought never occurred to me. I never knew I wanted to protect someone. I'd always rejected all that kind of masculine, pound-your-fists-against-your-chest kind of thought. I was trained to think it was anti-feminist. But in spite of my insecurities, my doubts, my own sadness and my raging need for a cigarette, I pulled her to me and wrapped my arms around her.

She turned around in my arms to face me. Her slight frame relaxed into the embrace, and her face rested against my chest.

Cece squeezed me tightly. 'Jay, Mrs. Catt also said I'd be here to help you too.'

10

I liked how she made me feel. I felt like rising to the occasion for her. I felt like I could.

We'd come back to the apartment after stopping at Watson's one more time for another round of turkey sandwiches to go. We sat on the floor of the apartment.

'Crisscross applesauce,' she said. She laughed as I tried to fold my body into a pretzel.

'So,' she said, 'why'd she leave?'

'Margot? I'm not really sure.'

Cece didn't go for it. She just raised an eyebrow. 'Really?'

I laughed at how dumb it was to say that. 'No, not really. I guess I know exactly why she left, I just don't like to talk about it.'

'Oh,' she said in with a sympathetic voice. But then instantly she changed her tone. 'Oh well, too bad. Shoot.'

I took a deep breath and I decided it might feel good to get it off my chest. 'I think she left because I couldn't be who she wanted me to be. I'm not an adventurer. I bored her. I may have almost killed her spirit.'

'That's a bit drastic. I'm sure you didn't kill her spirit,' Cece said, but from her expression I could tell she wondered if it was true. She didn't want to believe it was possible to kill someone's spirit.

'I think it's true. I think she had to leave before it was too late.'

She pondered the thought. Then, without a hint of restraint, she reached over to grab the pickle out of my Styrofoam container. She took a big bite and held it up. 'Sorry,' she said, as a slight look of embarrassment blushed her cheeks. 'I noticed you didn't eat your pickle at lunch.'

I didn't say anything. I just reached over and took her discarded tomatoes.

She smiled. 'What if it hadn't been

you? What if someone else found that camera, printed those pictures and brought me here?' Her tone brought my attention away from shoving her tomatoes into my sandwich to her eyes.

'I'm so glad it was you,' she said.

'But it wasn't me; I mean, I didn't do it.' My denial was instinctual, a purposeful avoidance of blame for an occurrence so life-altering it would forever change Cece's life. But it was also out of shame because I knew I wouldn't have done it — I wouldn't have had the courage. 'Mrs. Catt did this,' I said, a tone of defeat in my voice.

'Mrs. Catt may have started it, but you had the pictures printed and you hoped me here.'

She was right. I had hoped her here. I had desperately wanted her to be here. I don't like owning up to my mistakes. Isn't that terrible? Who knows that about themselves and just admits it like that? But it's true. I pass the buck. But with Cece it felt futile. I didn't even want to dodge responsibility, even though I was pretty sure I couldn't have been responsible, not fully anyway.

'I'm so sorry. I didn't do it intentionally — not that that matters much.'

'Honestly, Jay, I don't think it could've happened if I didn't want it to. I think we both wanted this.'

I wanted to believe that when she said *this*, she meant me. But she didn't have my picture. She didn't have a glimpse of what she would find behind the door to my apartment. She had a key, a key that could have led her to anyone.

'You wanted this — a different life. I wanted you.'

She reached over and touched my cheek. 'You wanted the happy you saw in those photos. But that wasn't real.'

'Are you real?'

'Oh, Jay,' she said, shaking her head.

It wasn't an answer, and I wasn't convinced this wasn't a dream or perhaps a hallucination. One in which I could go an entire day without a cigarette or the ache in my chest for Margot. Would I wake up in the morning to an empty house and a new ache? I wanted to believe I was this lucky. I wanted to believe there was magic in this situation; that this treasure had come into my life through the meddling of the crazy woman from Milford. I wanted to believe there weren't any details to figure out. I wanted to believe there weren't people missing her. Would we have to talk about it? She wasn't a lost puppy.

She leaned back and laid herself on the floor, her legs still twisted together. She raised her arms over her head. 'What would Margot and Joey do with this situation? Maybe we should take a lesson from them. They weren't all bad.' She was looking up at the ceiling; my eyes were on her and I let the question hang in the air.

11

We stood at the foot of the bed. It still had the duvet Margot had chosen, pastel-yellow and gray flowers all over it, and six pillows. His-and-hers night-stands flanked either side. Margot wanted our nightstands to reflect our personalities and she wanted us to choose each other's. Even at the time, I knew it was a giant trap. I knew she'd come home with the perfect item, the perfect piece of furniture to reflect my personality. I knew I'd fail and come home with yet another reason for her to be disappointed.

We spent a whole day shopping separately then set up our discoveries. We covered them with sheets, and pulled them off at the same moment for the big reveal. She pulled her sheet off to reveal a tom drum on a stand. It held a clock, a picture of the two of us, and a box of orange-flavoured Tic Tacs, my go-to I'm-quitting-again mints. She'd nailed it.

'Wow, that's incredible,' I had said. 'That's actually perfect. How do you do that?'

'I know, right? I saw this drum and thought of you instantly. The photo is your favourite one of us and the candy (she refused to call the orange Tic Tac mints) was a no-brainer.' She gave me a hug and a kiss on my cheek. 'I'm so glad you like it. Okay, now it's your turn. Go.'

I took a deep breath and steadied myself. I pulled the sheet off to reveal a vintage wrought iron and glass garden cart. It had ivy details welded onto the side and a decoratively coiled handle. It was a little more feminine that she usually liked but it was old, and since she seemed to be so fond of antique stores I thought it would be the perfect thing. She was always lamenting the fact that we didn't have a garden so I placed a plant on it and a glass for water; she was always thirsty at night.

She stared at it for a moment too long. I had failed. 'I don't get it. Is the water for the plant?' I looked over at the glass and suddenly felt stupid. Of course that's exactly what it looked like.

'No, no, it's for you. You're always thirsty at night. And the plant is because you've always wanted a garden.'

'A vegetable garden,' she said.

'Oh.'

'Where did you find that . . . I don't even know what to call it — a cart?'

'It's a garden cart, a vintage one. You love vintage stuff.'

'Yeah, but that's not what I mean when I say that.'

'For crying out loud, Margot. Why do you do this? You knew I couldn't pull this off. Do you like to be disappointed?' My voice was borderline yelling. I was so tired of letting her down.

'Forget it,' she said.

'No, let's not forget it.'

'Fine. I just thought that you knew

me better than that.' She pointed to the cart. 'Who did you buy that for? Because it certainly wasn't me.'

I flashed my disingenuous smile, the one she hated, and shook my head a little so the sarcasm wouldn't be missed. 'Stupid, I'm so stupid,' I said. 'I knew how this would go, and I walked right into it.' I strode over to the cart and grabbed the plant and water.

'What are you doing?' She was yelling now too.

'Starting over.'

'No, wait, it's fine.'

I marched past her and out of the apartment. I threw the plant and the glass of water down the trash chute.

'Jay!'

'What?' I spat out. I was standing in front of the chute, my hand still on the handle.

'You just killed that plant.'

I looked at her and realized I was throwing a tantrum. I felt like an idiot. I let go of the trash chute and stood there in exhausted defeat.

'I'm sorry. I'm sorry I disappointed you. I wish I was better at knowing you.'

She walked over and threw her arms around my waist. It was the end of the fight and nothing was resolved. The cart stayed though.

Now, two hundred and fourteen days later, Cece and I were standing at the foot of the bed with the awkward decision of who sleeps where.

'That's a lot of pillows.'

'Yeah, Margot wanted the bed to look complete.'

She turned her head to the side. I could tell she was trying to figure out what *complete* meant.

'Do you just throw them on the floor to sleep?' she asked.

'Well, I throw mine on the floor. But Margot always lined hers up nice and neat against the wall.'

'Hmm,' she said, nodding as if she was beginning to understand what Margot was all about. 'I like the cart. It needs a plant though.'

'Yeah,' I said, stifling a laugh, 'that's a long story.' Then it struck me. 'I can't believe it.'

'What?'

'Margot was right.'

'About what?'

'Margot said I bought this cart for someone else. She said it wasn't for her. She was right. I think I bought it for you.'

Cece took hold of my hand. 'I love it,' she said.

12

I gave Cece one of my Hanes tees. She came out of the bathroom and the shirt draped down to her knees. I'd changed into a pair of old gym shorts and silently said a prayer that I'd washed them. They didn't appear to smell badly, but I didn't trust myself to be able to smell my own filth, and there had been a few weeks there, after Margot left, that I just didn't have the energy or desire to get down to the laundry.

We stood awkwardly in my room, the bed looming large between us. 'So, you can sleep here and I'll sleep in the living room,' I said.

'On the couch?'

'Nah, I don't think that would work so well. I don't really fit on the couch. I'll just make a bed on the floor.'

She walked over to the bed and flung

herself across Margot's side. She patted the other side, an invitation for me to join her.

'Are you sure?'

'I don't want to be alone,' she said, in a voice that was barely above a whisper.

I let my body sink into the bed and felt her roll toward me from the shift in balance. I thought of a see-saw. 'Can I trust you to stay on your side?' I asked.

She giggled.

We were still and quiet in the darkness for so long that I assumed she was sleeping. I was startled when she spoke.

'What do you make of Pet?' she asked.

'I have no idea.'

'You know, I'd never seen a llama in person before the day I brought her the camera.'

'A llama?' I whipped my head in her direction. My eyes had adjusted to the darkness by then, and I could see her clearly. There was a small strip of light falling on her face from the separation in the curtains. She rolled onto her side and turned toward me. I was beginning to think sharing a bed was not such a great idea. I felt the heat fill the space between us and I was obsessing over my desire to touch her. I desperately wanted to feel her.

'I didn't meet a llama.' My voice cracked.

'The pig?'

The question broke my longing. I laughed. I laughed so hard I couldn't stop. She joined me.

'The cat?' she asked through her laughter.

'Yes! I did meet the cat. And also the dog, and the parrot.' Our laughter had not subsided. It was the kind of uncontrollable laughter that comes from exhaustion.

'Oh gosh, the parrot. It called me sweets,' she said.

We simultaneously sighed in high a whiny tone that indicates the laughter is dying down.

'Do you suppose they're all the same?

One Pet that keeps changing?' she asked.

'Yes.'

'Me too.'

'Do you suppose we're crazy?'

'Yes,' I said, as I rolled toward her. We were so close I could hear her eyelashes rub against the pillowcase when she blinked.

'They weren't wrong for leaving . . . were they?'

She was talking about Joey and Margot. 'I don't think so.'

I felt myself getting heavier and could hear her breathing settling into a slow heavy pattern. 'Cece?' My voice was rough and low.

'Hmm?' She sounded as though she was just moments from nodding off.

'I'm afraid to fall asleep. I'm afraid you'll be gone in the morning. Please be here when I wake up.'

She closed her eyes. 'I have nowhere else to go.'

It wasn't quite the response I wanted to hear. But I allowed it to comfort me.

'Jay?'

'Yeah?'

'I think I'm here — I think she sent me here, because it's where I want to be.'

That's it. That's what I wanted to hear.

13

I woke to the sound of clanking in the kitchen. A smile spread across my face, and I jumped out of bed. I smelled bacon before I reached the hallway. *She's an angel*, I thought.

I stood in the hall for a moment, leaning against the wall, watching her in the kitchen. She was humming a song by the band Rock Star Poet. 'Already in the kitchen cooking bacon for the man of the house. I like women from the sixties.'

She turned around and rolled her eyes. 'Women don't cook anymore?'

'Oh, I don't know, I suppose there are a lot who do. Margot didn't. We lived on take-out.'

'And is there some new law that states men can't cook for themselves in this decade?'

'When you cook as badly as me,

yeah, there should be a law against it.'

She got back to work on some potatoes cooking in a cast-iron skillet. 'Where did you get all this food?' I asked.

'I walked to the grocery store. I took money from your wallet,' she said, without a hint of apology, which I enjoyed.

'Wow, well, thanks.'

'Who said any of this was for you?'

I let her teasing pass. She went back to her song; then it occurred to me.

'How do you know that song?'

'Oh, that? It's just a little song that Joey had written . . . ' She stirred her potatoes slowly, obviously lost in thought. A sweet smile lit up her face. She was recalling a good memory. 'For me,' she said, 'he wrote it for me.'

I was stunned. 'Cece, Joey — your Joey — is Joey Monroe?'

'Yeah.' She whipped herself around.

'Holy . . . I can't believe it.'

'What! What?'

'Cece, he's a very famous guy.'

'What? What do you mean? You're kidding.'

I jumped up and grabbed my laptop.

'What's that?'

'It's a computer.'

'In your house?' Her shock registered all over her face.

'Yeah, they're everywhere now.'

'Wow. It's so . . . little.'

'Yeah.' I sat down and pulled up information about Joey. 'I thought you said he was an artist and photographer.'

'He was. I mean, he was really good and I always encouraged him to pursue his painting. But his first love was music. I didn't like it.'

'Why?'

'He wasn't himself when he was doing music. He would smoke too much weed, drink too much and just sit in Murphy's dirty, awful garage.'

'Murphy Gaines, the drummer? These were people in your life?' I was a huge fan of Murphy Gaines. I'd read every article about him ever written. I loved drums, although I'd never been any good at playing them.

'Yeah, not just *in* my life, they *were* my life. My world.'

'Look.'

I spun the laptop around to reveal a picture of Joey on stage in the 70s, his leather pants hanging low on his waist, his long hair stuck to his face, plastered there from sweat. He was touted as one of the godfathers of rock.

She sunk down into a chair to read the article. I hopped up to stir potatoes and flip bacon. The bacon sizzled and popped; bits of oil burned my skin. I watched her over my shoulder. Her pensive expression grew sadder with every paragraph. I reached over and scrolled down for her as she got to the end of the page. Her fascination with the computer was overshadowed by the feelings that were stirred by the story that unfolded in front of her.

It was all there: Joey's rise to fame as one of the most influential front men in the history of rock and roll, his struggles with drug addiction, the groupies, the fights, the womanizing, and his genius. A tear rolled down her cheek when she read the part about Murphy's overdose.

'Poor Murphy, he's always been a mess.' She spoke of him as though he were still someone in her life. 'Are there more in here?'

'Well, yeah, there's probably thousands on the internet; it's like a library that everyone can access from home at any time they want.'

'Fascinating.'

'I know.'

'I want to read more.'

I pulled up another article. It was about Joey in his life today. I turned off the stove and sat down next to her. It was an interview from a year ago, just a few months after Murphy's death.

*   *   *

Tunes Mag: So Joey, *will you be returning to the stage?*

Joey: Not without Murphy. I'm old

and rotten and filled with art and passion but my best friend is in the ground.

TM: Don't you think he'd want you to keep playing?

JM: (long pause) Yes. He was the force. There wouldn't have been a Rock Star Poet without him. You know, I think I'm going to return to photography or painting.

TM: Photography? Painting? The great Joey Monroe is an artist?

JM: Yeah, actually, I was pretty good.

TM: Why'd you choose music?

JM: (another long pause)

TM: Difficult question to answer?

JM: No, just a lost memory.

TM: The girl kind?

JM: The best girl. My model, my muse.

Joey laughs. His eyes light up.

TM: What's so funny?

JM: She was a funny girl. She hated the music, hated Murphy, hated the drugs. She wanted me to be an artist or *a photographer; wanted me to marry her.*

TM: What happened to her?

Joey takes a long drag on his cigarette.

JM: The music sent her away.

★ ★ ★

'Are you okay, Cece?'

She looked at me, tears streaming down her face. I pulled her to me and tucked her into my chest. 'It's okay.' *What a stupid thing to say, of course it's not okay,* I thought.

'Oh gosh, what a dope. I'm so sorry.' She pulled away but was still crying as she choked out her words.

'Cece, you don't need to apologize, it's fine. I mean, I can't even imagine what this must be like for you.'

'I don't know what it feels like either. I can't decide if I'm *broken*-hearted or *light*-hearted. I think it's both. I think I'm free. I know letting him leave . . . well, I suppose ultimately it wasn't my choice. I could have fought for him, gone with him, but I would've just been putting off the inevitable. We loved each other as we wanted each other to be, not for who we really were.'

The covering of her tears and the red rim of her eyelids made her blue eyes brighter. 'Cece, I'm so glad you are . . . ' I hesitated.

'What?'

I was nervous all of a sudden. I didn't want to screw this up. 'You. I'm so glad you didn't become what he wanted or needed you to be. I couldn't love that girl.'

She smiled and touched my cheek.

'Don't do that,' I said, my voice barely above a whisper.

'Why?'

'Because I will get the wrong idea.'

She smiled and before I could stop myself I bent down and kissed her. I wanted to feel her smile. Our kiss, which started out in tenderness, grew in intensity. I held her tightly, letting her presence dissolve the ache

I'd felt for two hundred and thirteen days.

When we parted she giggled. 'You snuck some bacon. Now whenever I eat bacon, I'll think of our first kiss.'

14

Cece spent the rest of the morning on the internet. She quickly learned how to scroll around and dig up information. She must have read countless articles about Joey and the band. I tried not to interrupt. I moved about the house and let her soak in the last forty years. I wondered what it must be like for her to see images of Joey now, as an old man. Considering the drugs and hard living, he'd actually aged well, but it must have been shocking to see him as he was and not as she remembered.

I went and sat out on the balcony and worried. I was a good worrier. I worried about Cece having to carry the burden of all these years dumping on her at once. Selfishly, I worried that she would have second thoughts about her choice to not follow him into his dream. I worried she wouldn't stay. I didn't want her to leave; I'd just found her. And then I worried that if she wanted to leave and couldn't she'd feel stuck. Stuck, like Margot had said she'd felt for over half of our relationship. I didn't want Cece to feel stuck.

Man, I could use a cigarette. I hadn't smoke since Cece had arrived. She was my own personal nicotine patch.

'How does anyone get anything done with that internet thing around?' Cece came out onto the patio. She sat down on Margot's chair, folding her legs underneath her like a little girl.

'There are many employers who are asking themselves that same question. It's a beautiful thing but also a giant time-suck.' I thought of Mr. Luu sneaking up on us at work. I think trying to catch us wasting time on the internet was his favourite game, his favourite way to waste his time.

'I expected to find you out here smoking.'

I was stunned. First, because I was really wishing I had one and was wondering if she'd read my mind, and second because I didn't realize she knew. 'How'd you know I smoked? I haven't had a single cigarette since you got here.'

'Well, your house isn't exactly the essence of fresh air.'

I winced from embarrassment. 'I guess I can't even smell it anymore. I think I quit though.'

'You *think*?'

'Yeah.'

'That's good. I think it can kill you.'

I just smiled.

'How are you?' I asked.

'I'm okay. Relieved.'

'Do you want to go home?'

She leaned her head back and closed her eyes. 'I can't explain it, but I guess Mrs. Catt knew what she was doing.'

'What do you mean?'

'Home. I've never felt so at home in my life.'

'What about your friends, family?'

'My parents died a week after my

eleventh birthday. They weren't really close to their families, in relationship or proximity, so I'd never really known any of them. I don't have any brothers or sisters, and my friends, well . . . I sort of screwed all that up when I started dating Joey. He became everything, all I ever needed. Like I said, he was my world.'

I took her hand but didn't say anything right away. I felt like I was pushing boulders around in my mind — organizing thoughts, deciphering code, and trying to figure out the appropriate phrase or words. I'm sure five full minutes went by before I finally spoke. 'I don't know what to say. I'm horrible in these situations.' And that's all I could come up with.

She looked at me without an expression. *I blew it*, I thought.

She closed her eyes again and rested her head. 'No, you're really not. You're perfect.'

'Do you want to go anywhere today?

We could go for a drive. I'm sure there are places you'd like to see.'

'I can't imagine doing anything better than this,' she said.

I love this woman.

15

I knew she wasn't perfect. I knew the situation was too fantastic, in a Fantasy Island sort of way, to be possible. It was too easy. I didn't do smooth sailing. Copacetic was not a word in my vocabulary.

We read the newspaper all morning, ate bacon, and drank coffee. I found myself periodically just staring at her, waiting for her to vanish.

'Jay, you're going to have to quit that.'

'What?'

'Staring.'

'I'm sorry. I'm just afraid you'll disappear.'

'I'm not going anywhere.'

Margot said that the first morning we woke up in this apartment. I told her we should stay in bed all morning. 'I can't today,' she'd said, 'but I'm not going anywhere. Another day.'

'I've heard that before,' I said.

'She had to leave, Jay, or I couldn't have come.'

I wondered if that was true. If Margot had never left, if I'd changed to make Margot stay, would Cece never have come? I knew I needed to stay in the moment and stop worrying about what would have happened or what would happen in the future. I knew the way you know how to solve someone else's problems. It's easy to look from the outside. I could see the mistakes I was already making. I was so afraid of this magic, that I was stamping it out like a flame instead of fostering it with soft breaths. I was beginning to realize that I was a suffocater — a person who suffocates another in relationships, that's me.

As I worried some more about my behaviour, my phone started vibrating against the table between us. I looked at the screen in disbelief. Margot.

Margot hadn't called me since she

left. I knew it wasn't necessary, but I started to feel guilty, like I'd been caught doing something I shouldn't. I froze, just staring at the vibrating phone.

'What is it doing?'

'Ringing.'

'Well, answer it.'

'It's Margot.'

'Oh.'

It could be that I was just seeing what I wanted to see. I wasn't really sure, and I certainly couldn't trust myself, but it seemed like she was disappointed. She turned her head and looked out over the balcony, as if to give me privacy. It buzzed again.

I don't know how many times it rang. I just let it buzz away. I think it only rings four times before going to the message, but for that moment in time, time seemed to stretch. I had an opportunity to figure out what I wanted. Did I want to talk to Margot? Had that phone rung just two days earlier, I would have thrown myself across the room to answer it. But today? Today I didn't have anything to say to Margot.

It finally stopped ringing. Cece and I looked at each other and knew we had both said goodbye to what had kept us from moving on with our lives. I leaned toward her and put one hand behind her head and gently brought her lips to mine. There was suddenly nothing I wanted more than to always be the one to kiss those lips.

16

One year later, Cece and I were walking down the street toward Watsons. It had become a routine, although we liked to think of it as tradition. Traditions are romantic; routines are, well . . . boring. And we'd decided that we're not boring. Every Saturday afternoon we ate turkey sandwiches on white, swapping her tomatoes for my pickles.

As we walked hand in hand, not thinking about how she came into my life or how I came into hers — we rarely talked about that anymore — I rubbed the back of her hand with my thumb.

We were just a few steps from the diner when a kid on a skateboard came rolling by. I instantly recognized him as the kid from the photo-mat.

'No Way!' he said as he rolled by and braced himself against the hood of a parked car. Cece and I stopped to make sure he was okay. 'Dude, you found her.'

Cece, who continued to dress herself in A-line dresses and ballet flats, looked at me, then at the kid, then back to me.

I laughed. 'Yeah, I think so.'

'That's awesome, dude. I had faith in you.'

I patted the kid on the shoulder. 'Thanks,' I said. Cece and I continued to walk on toward the restaurant. After a few steps we turned around to see a black cat walking down the sidewalk.

'Nah,' we said simultaneously, shaking our heads. 'Impossible.'

THE END

Other titles in the
Linford Romance Library:

ONE LAKELAND SUMMER

Teresa Ashby

Camping on a farm in the Lake
District following a successful business trip, young American Mike
Carter Junior sees the farmer's
daughter, Amy Palmer, for the first
time and falls instantly head-over-
heels in love. But Mike is due back
in the States, where his fiancée Kari
Reynolds is finalising the arrange-
ments for their wedding. Then Kari
travels to the Lakes to win her fiancé
back. Meanwhile, Mike's arrival has
set off a chain of events that could
well end in tragedy . . .

WITH LOVE FROM AUNT RUBY

Catriona McCuaig

When her engagement to Tom Carson is broken off, Alyssa Grant exchanges city life for an extended stay in the small Canadian town where her elderly Aunt Ruby is recovering from an injury. Ruby, a retired schoolteacher who is determined to set the world to rights, now has a new mission: to help her niece find her way back to happiness. Will Alyssa be reunited with Tom, or find a new love with Ruby's choice, handsome policeman Ben O'Hare?

WHERE MOONBEAMS DANCE

Rena George

Hannah Maxwell's gambler husband Brian dies suddenly from a brain hemorrhage, leaving her struggling to bring up her three children amidst a mountain of debt. Then a distant relative bequeaths to her a tidy sum, and the tenancy of a Highland croft. A stranger to the countryside, Hannah is determined to make a new life for her family — but brooding Ross Hunter, the estate manager, is less than welcoming. Yet Hannah finds herself increasingly drawn to him, and his help at the croft becomes indispensable . . .

SPECIAL MESSAGE TO READERS

THE ULVERSCROFT FOUNDATION
(registered UK charity number 264873)
was established in 1972 to provide funds for
research, diagnosis and treatment of eye diseases.
Examples of major projects funded by
the Ulverscroft Foundation are:-

- The Children's Eye Unit at Moorfields Eye Hospital, London
- The Ulverscroft Children's Eye Unit at Great Ormond Street Hospital for Sick Children
- Funding research into eye diseases and treatment at the Department of Ophthalmology, University of Leicester
- The Ulverscroft Vision Research Group, Institute of Child Health
- Twin operating theatres at the Western Ophthalmic Hospital, London
- The Chair of Ophthalmology at the Royal Australian College of Ophthalmologists

You can help further the work of the Foundation
by making a donation or leaving a legacy.
Every contribution is gratefully received. If you
would like to help support the Foundation or
require further information, please contact:

**THE ULVERSCROFT FOUNDATION
The Green, Bradgate Road, Anstey
Leicester LE7 7FU, England
Tel: (0116) 236 4325**

website: www.foundation.ulverscroft.com